Fix

Kwame Kwei-Armah won the ⁣ ⁣ ⁣ ⁣ ⁣ ⁣ ⁣ ⁣ ⁣ Award
for his first play, *Bitter Herb* (1998), which was subsequently
put on by the Bristol Old Vic, where he also became writer-
in-residence. He followed this up with the musical *Blues
Brother, Soul Sister*, which toured the UK in 2001. He co-wrote
the musical *Big Nose* (an adaptation of *Cyrano*) which was
performed at the Belgrade Theatre, Coventry, in 1999. In
2003 the National Theatre produced the critically acclaimed
Elmina's Kitchen, for which in 2004 he won the *Evening Standard*
and Charles Wintor Awards for Most Promising Playwright,
and was nominated for a Laurence Olivier Award for Best
New Play 2003. *Elmina's Kitchen* has since been produced and
aired on Radio 3 and BBC4.

Fire Up

Kwame Kwei-Armah

Fix Up

Methuen Drama

3 5 7 9 10 8 6 4 2

Published by Methuen Drama

Methuen Drama
A & C Black Publishers Limited
38 Soho Square
London W1D 3HB
www.acblack.com

First published in 2004 by
Methuen Publishing Limited

A CIP catalogue record for this book is available
from the British Library

ISBN-10: 0-413-77497-X
ISBN-13: 978-0-4137-7497-2

Typeset by Country Setting, Kingsdown, Kent
Printed and bound in Great Britain by
Cox & Wyman Ltd, Reading, Berkshire

Caution

Fix Up premiered at the National Theatre's Cottesloe
auditorium on 16 December 2004. The cast was as follows:

Brother Kiyi	Jeffery Kissoon
Carl	Mo Sesay
Kwesi	Steve Toussaint
Norma	Claire Benedict
Alice	Nina Sosanya
Director	Angus Jackson
Designer	Bunny Christie
Lighting Designer	Neil Austin
Music	Neil McArthur
Sound Designer	Gareth Fry

Fix Up

Characters

Brother Kiyi (pronounced 'key'), owner of the Fix Up Bookstore. An old fifty-five, with greying, unkempt locks.

Carl, thirty-five. A local 'care-in-the-community' delivery boy.

Kwesi, thirty. A militant Black activist who uses a room upstairs in the shop.

Norma, a part-time barber, preacher and photographer. She is Kiyi's best friend. Also fifty-five.

Alice, thirty-four. A beautiful but troubled visitor to the store.

Voices on Tape

Marcus Garvey, Jamaican-born leader of the American UNIA back-to-Africa movement of the early 1920s. Seen as the godfather of Black nationalism.

James Baldwin, celebrated and outspoken New York novelist, essayist and playwright.

Claude McKay, celebrated poet of the Harlem renaissance.

Scene One

Thursday, a late afternoon in early October. Outside is well cold.

It's Black History Month. We are in 'Fix Up', a small, old-school, 'Black conscious' bookstore. The place is much too small to hold the many shelves and bookcases that jam and squeeze up against each other. However, although at first sight the shop looks chaotic – no subject labels or even indicators – to the trained eye it is perfectly arranged. Starting at the shelf closest to the door, each subject is in alphabetical order, subdivided by genre, also in alphabetical order, followed by the authors, again in painstaking alphabetical order.

Sitting nobly on each and every bookshelf, almost as closely stacked together as the books, are African statues and carvings of giraffes, busts of great leaders, perfectly formed couples entwined, Ashanti stools, sculptured walking sticks, etc. Various Kentes and African cloths are hung on what little wall space there is left. Hanging from the ceiling in a less ordered fashion are a few dusty-looking male and female African outfits. Written over the door and above Brother Kiyi's till enclosure is a sign reading CLOSING DOWN SALE. *It is well old and dusty. On the floor, however, is a big black bin. The sign above that reads:* HELP KEEP US OPEN – ANY DONATION WELCOME.

Playing a little too loudly is a speech from the early Black leader Marcus Garvey. It is an old 1920s recording. As with all recordings of that period it's slightly sped up, but through the hiss we can hear the words clearly enough. Although his Jamaican accent is clear, we can hear Marcus is over-articulating in a 'Truemanesqe' style.

Voice of Marcus Should I openly help improve and protect the integrity of the black millions or suffer? I decided to do the latter. There is no future for a people that deny their past! My foreparents, my grandparents, my mother and fadder, did not suffer and die to give me an education so that I could discourage my people – because whatever education I acquired out of their sacrifice of over three hundred years, I shall use for the salvation of the four hundred million black people of the world. And the day that I shall forsake my people may God Almighty say, 'There is no more light for youuuuu!'

Buried beneath the counter – an enclosed, secure-looking box, big enough to fit maybe two people, somewhat to the right to the store – is **Brother Kiyi**, *fifty-five.* **Carl**, *thirty-five, happy by nature, enters through the front door. He is a care-in-the-community patient to whom all the local traders give a little carrying work, due to his obvious ambition to contribute. He is pushing a lorry driver's trolley with three boxes stacked on it. He looks around for* **Brother Kiyi**. *When he doesn't see him, he shouts out with his slight stammer in a loud cockney accent.*

Carl   Owiiii, 'cuse us mate, you sell rat-poison in here?

Still out of sight, **Brother Kiyi** *switches off the cassette and stops what he is doing. We hear his anger.*

Brother Kiyi (*as if speaking to someone off*)   Excuse me a minute.

We hear **Brother Kiyi** *boom. He has a refined but noticeable West Indian accent.* **Carl** *hides behind a shelf.*

Brother Kiyi (*angry*)   No! I do not sell rat-poison. Rat-poison is sold in the shop three doors down on the left. You'll find it behind the halal meat refrigerator and to the right of the well cheap airfares-to-the-subcontinent.

Now standing, **Brother Kiyi** *can't see the hidden* **Carl**. **Brother Kiyi** *is dressed in an African shaped Kente shirt on top of a thick woolly polo-neck with jeans. He has very long, greying locks. They are not hanging, but twirled on top of his head almost like a turban.*

Brother Kiyi   Hello! Hello!

Carl *is still hidden.*

Carl (*using cockney accent*)   No, I was definitely told the Fix Up Bookstore sold a whole load of rat poison . . .

Brother Kiyi   What? . . .

Carl *pops out, laughing.*

Carl (*changing back to his normal black London accent*)   Filling de yout' dem hea- hea- head wid rubbish!

Brother Kiyi *kisses his teeth, and pulls a vexed face.*

Brother Kiyi   You see you? When is stupidness you talking you don't have no stammer dough!

Carl (*still chuckling at his own gag*)   I love it! You get so ig- ig- ignorant when you're vex.

Brother Kiyi   Ignorant? How many times do I have to tell you, I am not ignorant! Ignorant is when you are not aware; I, on the contrary am aware . . .

Carl (*finishes off, quick and bored*)   . . . of the rightful place I hold in hi- hi- history . . .

Brother Kiyi   . . . because unlike the overwhelming majority of my people . . .

Carl   . . . I read . . .

Brother Kiyi   . . . digest and make manifest . . .

Carl   . . . the greatness of our heritage.

Brother Kiyi (*a positive acclamation*)   Iiiiiitchsss!

Carl   Wish I never said it now!

Brother Kiyi *runs back into his little box, bends down to the floor. We hear him speaking.*

Brother Kiyi   Hello, hello, yes! I'm terribly sorry, I've found it now . . . The order reference number is . . .

He stands with an very old-fashioned telephone in his hands. **Carl** *is looking at the books.*

Brother Kiyi   WA 23767. Brother Kiyi, Fix Up Bookstore, Tottenham N15. No, Brother is not my Christian name! The name on the order sheet should simply say – You know what? I have been waiting three weeks for what should have been here within ten days! Have you ever faced a crowd that's waiting for their history to arrive? . . . It has not been delivered!

Carl *has wheeled his trolley into view. He tries to point to the boxes on it, but can't catch* **Brother Kiyi***'s eye.*

Brother Kiyi   My friend, I am the only person that works here.

Carl *waves. Still no attention is being given to him.*

Brother Kiyi   If a parcel from Freight Line had been delivered today . . .

We can see that the boxes have 'Freight Line' written all over them.

Carl *starts to point to the boxes in an over-the-top manner.*

Brother Kiyi   It could only have been delivered to me!

Carl (*shouts*)   Brother Kiyi!

Brother Kiyi   Excuse me. (*Barks.*) What?

Carl   Are these dem?

Brother Kiyi *looks at the logo emblazoned all over the boxes. He goes back to the phone.*

Brother Kiyi   Madam, I may have to call you back! (*He puts down the phone.*)

Brother Kiyi   Carl. What are you doing with my delivery of − (*He calms himself.*) − with my delivery?

Carl   The brother was unloading his van, and that's my job, innit? Delivery! I saw it was for you, signed for it and bought them in. Bloody stinking parking warden was just about to give the man a ticket, you know? Delivering, you know, and was still gonna ticket him, you know?

Brother Kiyi   I figure I know, Carl.

Carl (*imitates shooting*)   Shotters for them.

Brother Kiyi *looks up sharply.*

Brother Kiyi   I don't believe he deserves to get shot for doing his job, Carl.

Carl You've changed your tune. When they introduced the red lines you said they were murdering you and dem deserve death!

Brother Kiyi Well, that was . . .

Carl When Mr Mustafar bought the freehold you said then, fire 'pon the weak hearts that didn't back you up . . . and when . . .

Brother Kiyi Yes, I get the message . . . (*Changes the subject to get out of it.*) That still no excuse for you to not tell me they reach!

Carl I tried to, but you know what you're like when you're focused on one ting. You shut out the rest of the w-w- world.

Brother Kiyi *comes swiftly towards the boxes. He approaches them with reverence.*

Brother Kiyi That's 'cos man is only suppose to do one ting at a time.

Carl What you talking about? Wh- when I'm with my gal, I does be stroking – (*Hip actions.*) – and feeling . . . (*Tuning in a radio for the breast action.*) Feels perfectly natural to be doing those two tings at the same time!

Brother Kiyi You never stutter when you're talking nastiness. (*Indicates to the boxes.*) Help me na!

Enter **Kwesi**, *thirty, good-looking.* **Brother Kiyi** *likes* **Kwesi**, *mainly because of his militant Black stance. He has a big box in his arms.*

He makes his way to the back of the store almost as if he doesn't want to say hello to **Brother Kiyi** *and* **Carl**.

Brother Kiyi Tende Mwari, Brother Kwesi.

Kwesi Tende Mwari.

Brother Kiyi They reach, you know, they reach! History, my friend, reach!

Kwesi   Great! Has anyone come here for . . .

Brother Kiyi   Yes, you've three friends upstairs waiting for you.

Kwesi   Thanks.

Brother Kiyi   Somalians? I don't know much about their history. What happen to Jamal, Eric and Ade?

Kwesi (*still trying to get away*)   Need people around you with backbone, know what I'm saying?

Brother Kiyi   Know what you're saying? I am surrounded by the most spineless punks this town has ever seen! Abrahams didn't want to sell, you know! We could have pressurise him not to sell. But no, it's every punk for himself.

Kwesi   That's Babylon. Later.

Brother Kiyi *looks at the box in his hands.*

Brother Kiyi   Big box?!

Kwesi (*slight beat*)   Computer from home. (*He leaves.*)

Carl, *who has had his back turned to* **Kwesi**, *now turns to lift the boxes and place them on the counter. In silence,* **Brother Kiyi** *opens a box and pulls out a thick, brown-bound book. It looks historic. He smiles, holds the book aloft almost as if about to raise it to the heavens.*

Carl   How much did they set you back?

Brother Kiyi   All I have . . . I feel like a child in a . . . (*Questioning his own lack of eloquence.*) Words, what are they, huh?!

He pulls out another book from the box, carefully opens and looks through it.

The telephone rings. Carefully **Brother Kiyi** *puts the book down and moves towards the telephone, still looking at the book.*

Brother Kiyi   Tende Mwari, how may I help you? . . . Mikel? . . . I see, I see . . . OK, Donna, calm down, just um, listen to me. You know the Law Centre on Peterdown Road? OK, go there, ask for Della, tell her I sent you, yes,

say brother Kiyi sent you and she'll see you immediately.
Is that OK? . . . Good. When you've left there come and
I'll have a book waiting that will educate you on the do's
and don'ts. Tende Mwari.

Carl Who was that?

Brother Kiyi Donna, young Mikel's mother. They want
to permanently exclude him from school. Pass me that book
there, please, yes, that one, bringing the black boy into
manhood . . .

Carl What did he do?

Brother Kiyi Caught smoking weed. Poor sister . . .
directly behind you, black and green cover. Yes that's the
one.

Carl *hands him the book.*

Brother Kiyi Good.

Carl I like it when those women come in here and talk to
you. Man, they look at you with respect and dat. You wanna
capitalise on that!

Brother Kiyi Never mix up the look of respect for love,
Carl. Heartache lies there.

*He methodically wraps up the book in brown paper and places it in a
plastic bag.* **Carl** *watches. When he has finished, he returns to his
new arrivals. He pulls another book from the box. He does this again
and again.*

Brother Kiyi Carl, you know what these are? Forget
Booker T, forget Langston Hughes! These are the great
voices of we past. (*He continues reading.*) Twelve volumes of, of
t- (*Struggles with word.*) – truth.

Carl You know you stutter when you moved?

Brother Kiyi (*joking*) Shut up!

Carl *decides to pick one up and read the title for himself. He struggles
with the words.*

Brother Kiyi   Careful!

Carl   *Sla- slave Nar- ra- tive . . .*

Brother Kiyi   . . . That's right, *Narrative* . . .

Carl   *Collection of Her Majes . . .*

Brother Kiyi   . . . *Her Majesty's . . .*

Carl   *Colonial Voices.*

Brother Kiyi (*sincerely, but pointed*)   Well done!

Carl   Yeah! What's all that about, then?

Brother Kiyi   In 1899 a group of social anthropologists went across the entire West Indies – British, French, Spanish, Dutch – and interviewed the last remaining beings that were enslaved. Two thousand, three hundred Africans that were between the ages of five and twenty-five when slavery was abolished. Most of them old like 'somum! But this is bondage, brother . . .

Carl *raises his eyebrows and smiles at the word bondage.*

Carl   Bondage, oh yeah?

Brother Kiyi   Come on now, don't be stupid.

Carl*'s face returns to studious enquirer.*

Brother Kiyi   This is the institution that bought us here, Carl, spoken about, written down in their own words, their dialect. That's always been the problem with slavery, see . . . We've been able to witness other people talking about their genocide, but ours, well, ours has been confided to saccharine American sagas or puerile political statement by people who don't give an blast about we!

Carl   Can I be frank? I don't know what the arse you're talking about.

Brother Kiyi (*laughs, catching himself about to preach*)   Haaaaa. At last, this is the human connection, Carl. Maybe if more of the youth could hear, see where they've come from, they'd have a little bit more respect for where they are.

Carl   Seen. Look, gotta go, all this deep talk is making me sick. Mr Dongal, from the halal butcher's wants me to run down to the abattoir with him. First time. Neat, huh?

Brother Kiyi   We'll do your reading when you come back then.

Carl (*sings to himself as he leaves*)   The main reason me like it from behind, you can reach under me belly, rub me clit same time!

Norma *enters.*

Norma   What nastiness is that?

Carl   Sorry, Auntie Norma.

Norma (*sharp on him*)   Stop that auntie-ting. People will think we is family.

Carl   But we are family! The African family. What Marcus say, every black man is an African, innit, Brother Kiyi?

Brother Kiyi (*pleased, he smiles*)   Exactly, Carl.

Norma   I'm not related to no crack addict!

Brother Kiyi   Norma!

Carl   Former! . . .

Norma   Hard love, Kiyi, hard love.

Brother Kiyi *shakes his head, pulls out a book from the box, an old, thick, bound book.*

Carl   Later. (*He exits.*)

Norma   So they reach?

Brother Kiyi (*pleased*)   Yeah, man.

Norma   Good, good.

Brother Kiyi *undoes his locks and shakes them out.* **Norma** *looks at* **Brother Kiyi**'s *hair.*

Norma   Boy, don't shake that ting at me. One sumting I don't like, that Rasta ting you have on you head. And that alien hair you have on your head is better.

Brother Kiyi   It don't have nothing to do with no Rasta . . .

Norma   I don't care about you symbol of rebellion stupidness. It look nasty. You wash it?

Brother Kiyi   Yes, Norma, is wash me wash me head. You happy now?

Norma (*changes subject*)   Na man, vex me vex. I sit down in front the television nice and comfortable, ready to watch me dog dem run, when the husband come in a start to harangue me soul.

Brother Kiyi   What he want?

Norma   Sex, innit? No, he want me to run out the road to buy some cowfoot and pig trotters. I know you doesn't like me to buy from dem people next door, but Dongal and dem is the only place man could find a decent home food. Not one of dem black shop close to me have anything to make old West Indians happy.

Brother Kiyi (*slightly distracted*)   That they don't sell that kinda slave food is what makes this West Indian happy.

Norma (*emphatic*)   My grandfather used to eat cowfoot and there was nothin' slave about him! Except maybe him name.

Brother Kiyi   Which was what?

Norma   George de Third!

Norma *goes round into the box and carefully pulls out a draughts board. The pieces are still on it.*

Norma   You looking damn thin, you know, boy? You use all you corn to pay Mustafar he money, innit?

Brother Kiyi *doesn't reply, just smiles slightly.*

Norma   I making a broth tonight, come over na?

Brother Kiyi (*a little nervous*)   Thanks, but I'll pass on the hog!

Norma (*plays back* **Brother Kiyi**'s *reaction to the money question*)   You have paid him, haven't you?

Beat.

Brother Kiyi   Abrahams always use to give me a month or two bligh! Why should I pay as soon as he ask for it?

Norma   Because Abrahams doesn't own the place any more. Mustafar does.

Brother Kiyi   What's wrong with our people, eh, Norma? The Jewish man come here and buy up the place, then a next immigrant come and buy it off him. Leapfrogging the West Indian. What was wrong wid we, eh?

Norma   A black landlord would ah let you off you rent?

Brother Kiyi   That's not the point.

Norma   All I know is, Kiyi, you owe the man he rent. Pay you rent.

Brother Kiyi   I can't. I spend all me money.

Norma   On woman?

Brother Kiyi (*pointing to bookshelves*)   What need do I have of a woman when I have Morrison, Macmillan and Walker?

Norma   Dem don't bring you cocoa in bed or bury you when you dead. Woman is the only excuse I'll accept. But you've spent it on the books, innit? You promised me you wouldn't do that. You promised.

Brother Kiyi   Oh Norma, I saw these in the catalogue and I couldn't resist them.

Norma   And if you don't pay the man you money you'll be resisting the wind and the rain on the blasted streets! He's only looking for an excuse, Kiyi!

Brother Kiyi (*gets arrogant*) He'll just have to wait. That's it.

Norma You know what? Talking to you is only going to get my diabetes up. I have time for three moves.

Brother Kiyi (*re unpacking books*) Norma, I'm doing something important!

Norma That's right, losing. It's time me beat you rah, I mean it's time for me to take my victory! I can smell it.

Brother Kiyi What nonsense you talking? . . .

Norma Don't be hiding behind no books. When it's licks time, it's licks time.

Brother Kiyi Come, three moves and that's it. (*He goes over to the board.*)

Norma (*perfectly straight face*) Is my move, innit!

Brother Kiyi (*pulls a piece of paper from his back pocket*) Whose signature is this?

Norma Mine.

Brother Kiyi And what does it say?

Norma (*reluctantly*) Kiyi has the next move.

Brother Kiyi Thank you. (*He looks over the board slowly.*) You see, nothin' like the power of de pen, girl.

They start to play. **Norma** *looks across at the books.*

Norma How much of dem book you get?

Brother Kiyi (*slightly embarrassed*) You back on that? Three sets twelve.

Norma Three sets of twelve!

Brother Kiyi (*beat*) And another two sets are on order, when I get a little money.

Norma (*disbelief*) You don't have money for food, and you ordering two sets ah books?

Brother Kityi (*quote voice*) I'm forced to believe that we can survive whatever we must survive. But the future of the Negro in this country is precisely as bright or as dark as the future of the country. Jimmy Baldwin, 1963.

Norma *makes her move.*

Norma I bet James wasn't bloody hungry when he wrote that. King me, you bitch!

Brother Kiyi For a woman of the cloth . . .

Norma Part-time!

Brother Kiyi . . . your language is very colourful.

Norma Don't try dem dirty tactics to put me off. Watch you moves, not my language.

Brother Kiyi Oh, of that you can be sure.

Norma *realises that her king has been blocked in.*

Norma Ahhhhhhh, man. How could you block in me king so?

Brother Kiyi By watching the game.

There's a moment of silence.

Norma (*looks at her watch*)   Rah, last move. (*She makes it.*) Scamp. Deal wid dat!

Brother Kiyi Ummmm.

Norma Haaaaaa. You see!

She starts to sing a church song, dancing.

Norma
   Victory is mine, victory is mine,
   Victory today is mine.
   I told the devil get thee behind,
   Victory today is mine.

(*Switches back to serious speech.*) I have to go.

Brother Kiyi Eh! Sign the paper.

Norma   Sign it for me na! You know me handwriting not too good.

Brother Kiyi   You too damn lie. Is challenge you want to challenge me when you come back. Sign the ting!

Norma (*smiles*)   Alright. (*She writes it down.*)

Norma   Brother Kiyi has the next move.

Brother Kiyi   Date!

Norma   15th October.

Brother Kiyi   Iiiiech!

Norma *signs, then, just before she goes to the door, takes a tenner out of her pocket and gives it to* **Brother Kiyi**.

Brother Kiyi   Na man, it's alright. I'm alright. Seriously.

Norma   Shut you mouth.

Brother Kiyi   Is not you that tell me you can't afford to pay you light bill the other day?

Norma   Take the ting.

Brother Kiyi   You could do me a favour, though?

Norma   What?

Brother Kiyi *takes a letter from his back pocket.*

Brother Kiyi   Just got this letter and I don't fully understand it. Could you ask you daughter to look over it for me?

Norma   Thought Della does your legal tings?

Brother Kiyi   She's got a lot of work on at the moment. I don't want to burden her.

Norma (*recognises the lie*)   You mean you owe her too much? No big ting. I go give Paulette when she come over this evening. (*Before she exits, she turns and says:*) I love you, yuh na brother, but – (*Points to the books.*) – you too stubborn for your own good.

Brother Kiyi (*calling after her*)   Where are we without hope?
Say hello to Bernie. And tell him to stop cook de master
throw-offs!

Norma   I'll tell her that when you cut you hair!

She moves off and starts to look at the bookshelves near the back.

Brother Kiyi *looks through another book. Suddenly he springs up
and begins to search for a space to place the books. After much
deliberation he decides to take down a row of modern black love stories.*

Brother Kiyi (*talking to himself*)   Stories of black love.
I wonder how that differs from say stories of white love? (*He
kisses his teeth.*) It's got to be you, I'm afraid.

*He takes down the books and, carefully brushing down the shelf, places
the new ones in their place, in a prominent place in the shop. Pleased
with himself, he pulls one of the books down and reads aloud to
himself. The lights slightly fade, as if we are in the world of his head.
He reads in the voice of the storyteller, but without comment.*

Brother Kiyi   'My name is Shang Harris and I live in
Port of Spain, Trinidad. Dey love fe talk about de niggers
dem stealin'. Well you know what de fust stealin' done? Hit
was in Afriky, when de white folks stole de niggers jes' like
you'd go get a drove o' hosses and sell 'em. Dey'd bring a
boat down dere wid a red flag, 'cos dey knowed dem nigger
people love bright colours, and when dey see it dey'd follow
it till dey got on de boat. Den when it was full o' niggers,
dey'd bring 'em over here and sell 'em. Welcome Shang to
my humble abode.'

The lights come back up. **Brother Kiyi** *exhales. Reading about
slavery saddens him to his core. He stops reading just as the door to the
bookstore opens and in walks* **Alice**, *thirty-four, mixed race.* **Brother
Kiyi** *pulls the book back up as if reading again, but he is not. He is
slightly taken by her attractiveness.*

Alice   Hi.

He does not reply. She moves a little closer tries again.

Hello?

He looks up from the book and smiles a little smile.

Brother Kiyi   Tende Mwari.

She pauses for a second, desperately trying to remember the proper response. She can't.

Alice   What does that mean?

Brother Kiyi   Well, in the ancient language of Kwaswahili, it is the greeting that one villager would give to the other.

Alice   Right, that bit I get, but what does it mean?

Brother Kiyi   As you know, translations are always notoriously inaccurate . . .

Alice   But? . . .

Brother Kiyi   Roughly translated, it means 'Hello' . . .

Alice (*trying to remember*)   And I say in return? . . .

Brother Kiyi   It's very difficult, I wouldn't worry yourself about it!

Alice (*slightly pissed at his dismissal*)   Right.

He returns to the book. She returns to looking at the bookshelves.

Alice   It's Black History Month, isn't it?

Brother Kiyi   Indeed it is.

Alice   Must be a good time for business, eh? Bet everyone like me comes in looking for something that will broaden their understanding of, well, black history. What do you recommend, Brother Kiyi?

Brother Kiyi   Well, young lady . . .

Alice   I don't know about the 'young lady'. According to my mother, at thirty-four I should have been married, at least once, and had my one-point-six children years ago.

Brother Kiyi   Your mother's from where?

Alice (*she gets a little defensive*)   Oh, um, she's English, from up north.

Brother Kiyi   Oh.

Alice   Why do you ask?

Brother Kiyi   It's a very Caribbean thing to say, that's all. My mother had me when she was twenty-seven, and I'm the last of six.

Alice   Wow, what age did you start?

Brother Kiyi   Me? I don't have any children. To the profound disappoint of my mother.

Awkward silence.

Alice   I'm sorry?

Brother Kiyi   Nothing to be sorry about. I chose to over-share.

But he returns to his book and she to the shelves. He turns the Marcus Garvey tape back on. Marcus is in full-throttle mode. It is a passionate oration.

Voice of Marcus   Africa has been sleeping, not dead. You can enslave for three hundred years the body of a man, you can shackle the hands of men, you can shackle the feet of men, you can imprison the body of men, but you cannot shackle or imprison the minds of men . . .

We hear the wild audience response to Marcus. **Alice** *tries to break the silence.*

Alice   Who is that speaking?

Brother Kiyi *turns it down a tad.*

Brother Kiyi   The Honourable Marcus Garvey.

Alice (*excited*)   Wow, I'll have one of those, please.

Brother Kiyi   The cassette is my own personal property, but if you go to the other aisle, on the top shelf you'll see many of his books.

Alice (*as she does so*)   Are his books any good?

Brother Kiyi   Well, er, I seem to think so!

Alice   Great! Then I'll buy 'em!

Brother Kiyi (*slightly suspicious*)   There are a few! You might want to start with one.

Alice   Actually I don't so much as read but have one of those photographic memories. I kind of scan it and it goes in. (*She picks up two books and goes to the counter.*) I'll have these two. Thank you.

Brother Kiyi   Good.

He methodically puts the books in a brown bag, writes the sales in a little black book and hands the bag to her.

Brother Kiyi   That will be £46.75, please.

She hands him her card.

Brother Kiyi   Sorry, we don't have the facility to process cards. Cash or cheques only. But cash is always best.

Alice (*trying hard*)   Good thing I bought my cheque book out with me.

She writes it out while he watches. She hands him the cheque and the card.

Brother Kiyi *looks at the signature for a while.*

Brother Kiyi   Do you have any other type of identification on you?

Alice (*taken aback*)   Why?

Brother Kiyi   The signature is, well, is a little different on the cheque.

Alice   Let me see. Well, it doesn't look that different to me.

He doesn't respond.

Maybe it's a little untidy but I always write fast when I'm nervous.

Brother Kiyi   What do you have to be nervous about?

Alice (*stutters for a second*)   I didn't actually mean nervous, I meant excited.

He stares at her blankly.

Alice (*as if saying 'dooooh'*)   New books!

Brother Kiyi   I see.

Alice (*only just containing her vexation*)   Here's my driver's licence. Picture's a bit old, but hey, same chick.

He looks at it for a while, then holds it out so that she can take it from his hand. She doesn't.

Brother Kiyi   Sorry about that, but one has to be careful.

Alice   One?

Brother Kiyi   Yes.

She calms. She takes the cheque card and the books.

Alice   Thank you. (*She walk to the door.*) By the way, I don't know about Kwaswahili, but in real Swahili one responds to 'Hello' with 'Habari Yako'.

Brother Kiyi   Is that so? How do you know that?

Alice (*feeling slightly triumphant*)   I had an East African boyfriend. Once.

Brother Kiyi   Thank you for telling me that.

Alice   It's OK. I wanted to over-share.

He waits for her to open the door.

Brother Kiyi   Safi. (*Swahili.*)

Alice *turns around slightly embarrassed and then leaves.*

Brother Kiyi *turns Marcus back up and starts to read his slave narrative again.*

Voice of Marcus   If black people knew their glorious past then they'd be more inclined to respect themselves . . .

Fade out.

Scene Two

Fix Up Bookstore. Three days later. **Brother Kiyi** *sits reading the slave narratives. Enter* **Norma**. *She is wearing a different wig from the last time we saw her.*

Brother Kiyi   Hey girl.

Norma   Don't 'Hey girl' me, you stubborn old fool!

Brother Kiyi   What I do you now?

Norma   The letter you asked me daughter Paulette to look at.

Brother Kiyi   Yeah?

Norma   What don't you understand about if you don't pay your rent within twenty-one days Mustafar is going to send in the bailiffs? Dated twenty days ago!

Brother Kiyi   I understand it all. What I want to find out is what I can do about it.

Norma   You call Della! Get her to inform them you going to pay!

Brother Kiyi   Ah, Della's great, but she don't have the stamina I require for this battle.

Norma   You mean she has grown tired ah you?

Brother Kiyi   *(kisses his teeth)*   What Paulette say?

Norma   That you need to pay! Like today! –

Brother Kiyi *kisses his teeth again.*

Norma   You know what the problem with you is? You think the world is waiting on you, Kiyi! Well, it's not. While you're sitting in here being obstinate, Mustafar is moving forwards. Didn't I tell you to meet me at the town hall last night?

Brother Kiyi   I was busy.

Norma My backside you were busy! All the other lease-holders were there!

Brother Kiyi I don't go anywhere dem punk rockers will be. If they'd have stood by me in the first place none of this would have been happening!

Norma That is history, Kiyi.

Brother Kiyi (*irate*) No my friend, *his story* are the fables of his winnings. (*Points to the slave narrative books.*) This is history. Anyway, it wasn't telling me anything I didn't know already.

Norma Oh, so you know that he plans to turn the places above you into luxury flats? What do you think is gonna happen next?

Brother Kiyi They'll pretty up the front, give me a new sign.

Norma Which one of them young rich children parents you think gonna loan dem child money to buy flat on top of an extreme black political bookshop? He has to get you out.

Brother Kiyi Norma, me know all of that. Me even know he plan to replace my bookstore with shop that sells black hair products.

Norma How do you know that?

Brother Kiyi Two people came in here yesterday to measure up!

Norma To measure up?

Brother Kiyi Yes. But he's messing with the wrong guy. I'm gonna talk to my MP. I'm gonna start a petition, speak to all the local black celebrities . . .

Norma I wouldn't count on them if I were you.

Brother Kiyi You can't replace history with hair gel.

Norma   Kiyi, our MP was there. Smiling. Agreeing. Saying thank you. The only good ting about that meeting is that they asked me to talk. Dem requested that a community man like myself make comment on dem plans.

Brother Kiyi   What you say?

Norma   I said I was outraged.

Brother Kiyi   And?

Norma   If you were bloody well there you'd have known what I said! We can't mek dem run roughshod over us like that man. Anyway, I went to the doctor this morning and you know what he tell me?

Brother Kiyi   You diabetes getting worse?

Norma   Me diabetes getting worse. In fact they might have to take off the foot. This go take me to me premature grave.

Brother Kiyi   Hey, girl, don't talk stupidness!

Norma   Listen, if me ah go dead, when me reach de fadder gate, I want to be able to look he in the eye and say, 'Lord, I did do something down there!' (*Beat.*) So I went to the bank. There was three grand in it. Here's two. Pay the man.

Brother Kiyi   DON'T BE STUPID.

Norma   TAKE IT. I understand where you coming from, man, but you can't fight this from where you are, Kiyi. You need help. Now take this, pay the man. Pay me back when you can.

Brother Kiyi   Norma, you know that's not possible. Listen to me good. If I pay the man his money now, he's gonna expect it on time every quarter. My business doesn't run like that!

Norma   And neither does his!

Brother Kiyi   I always square up by end of year! What's wrong wid dat?

Norma   It's unreasonable, Kiyi.

Brother Kiyi   And so is the offer of your savings. I can't take it.

Norma   Kiyi, though I don't agree with all you stupidness, you love black. And all of my life I have been taught to fear it, I hate it, to cuss it. That ain't right! Take the money. Anyway, if you go I have nowhere to play draughts. Take it. Please.

She holds out her hand with the envelope. **Brother Kiyi** *reluctantly takes it.*

Brother Kiyi   Don't think that go stop me whipping you backside.

Norma   Phone him now. Tell them you coming!

Brother Kiyi   Now?

Norma   Now.

Brother Kiyi *picks up the phone.*

Brother Kiyi (*with smile*) Just 'cos you give me little money you think you could boss me around? (*Serious switch.*) Hello, put me through to Mr Mustafar, please . . . Who's calling? His nemesis . . . No, that's not all one word . . . Thank you . . . Mustafar, Kiyi here. You think you catch me, innit? Well you lie. I coming with you money . . . Three? I think I can just about make that. Cool.

He slams down the phone.

Norma *smiles.*

Enter **Kwesi**, *with a box in his hands.* **Brother Kiyi** *puts the envelope of money away.*

Brother Kiyi (*bouncing back*)   Tende Mwari, Brother Kwesi.

Kwesi (*not reciprocating* **Brother Kiyi**'s *joyous tone*)   Tende Mwari, Sister Norma.

The narratives catch **Kwesi**'s *eye. He stops to look.*

Norma   Kwesi!

She walks off and starts to look at the bookshelves near the back.

Brother Kiyi (*remains positive*)   So, how's the revolution today?

Kwesi (*indicating upstairs*)   Fine, my brother. I'm off up!

He is about to walk past **Brother Kiyi** *to the room upstairs when* **Brother Kiyi** *stops him.*

Brother Kiyi   Hey, I just read that Michael Jackson has been a signed-up member of the Nation of Islam for ten years?

Kwesi   How can you have the most prominent manifestation of black self-hate as a member? Char! Michael should have been shot the moment he bleached his skin.

Brother Kiyi   So what happen? A brother can't look a little forgiveness?

Kwesi   Can you forgive slavery? Can the European repent for that?

Brother Kiyi *is quiet.*

Kwesi   Only thing this world understands, Kiyi, power. And until we have that, no matter what we have up there – (*Pointing to head.*) – we're all joking it.

Brother Kiyi   What you gonna build if you don't know where you're coming from? I built mine (*Re his books.*), you gotta build yours.

Kwesi   For real. (*He makes to go.*)

Brother Kiyi (*grabbing the opportunity*)   Brother Kwesi, I tried to go into the room upstairs yesterday, but the door was locked.

Kwesi   Yeah, that's right. Sorry, I forgot to tell you. But it's OK, I've got the key.

Brother Kiyi   There's never been a key for that lock!

Kwesi   Oh, at last week's meeting we . . . we changed the locks. The new computers and that. I'm so sorry, we should have informed you but what with all this march and all, it must have slipped my mind.

Brother Kiyi (*smiling*)   Right.

Pause.

Kwesi   I'll do a copy and get it right to you?

Brother Kiyi   Fine.

Norma *comes back to the front.*

Norma   Kiyi, where is those black love books? They're very lovely, you know!

Enter **Carl**. *He is carrying a box of provisions.*

Carl   Brother Kiyi, I ain't got but five minutes so we need to hit it straight away.

He sees **Kwesi** *and stops at the door.*

Kwesi (*can't resist a dig*)   Hey, Brother Carl, are you coming on the march?

Brother Kiyi (*innocently*) I'm not your brother, and which march is that?

Kwesi   The Reparations for Slavery march we've organised.

Brother Kiyi   No, I don't think so.

Carl *is still standing at the door.*

Kwesi (*gets vexed*)   You, a recipient of state brutality, can't find one hour out of your day to march for our people's right to be repaid! That's why our race is going nowhere fast. I'm upstairs, Brother Kiyi. (*He exits.*)

Norma   I tired tell you I don't like that boy, you know. You want me to come with you at three?

Brother Kiyi   Na man. I cool.

Norma   Alright, I gone. Later, dutty boy!

Norma *exits.*

Carl *comes up to the noticeboard next to the till enclosure and reads the poster.*

Carl   Why is he always so angry?

Brother Kiyi   He's a serious young man.

Carl   Do you reckon his face is vex like that when he's doing it?

Carl *demonstrates sex doggy-style with a vexed face.*

Carl   Huh! Huh! Huh! Take it, baby!

Brother Kiyi *kisses his teeth. Enter* **Alice**, *who crosses* **Norma** *at the door.* **Alice** *has her headphones on, and we can hear the music blasting. Her face looks vexed or at least determined. Both men look up at her, embarrassed. She smiles and starts to look at a bookshelf.* **Carl** *decides to continue.*

Carl   It ain't natural, is it, brother? There's too much fun to be had in this world to be vex all the time. What you saying, sister?

He walks up to **Alice** *and taps her on the shoulder.*

Alice   Pardon?

Carl   Are you one of those reparation-marching, hard-faced, straight-talking conscious types?

Alice   I don't think so!

Carl   I knew it. I could see you were different from your hair! You mixed people ain't stupid!

Alice *doesn't know what to say.*

Carl   I'm Carl.

Alice   Alice.

Carl   Come on, Brother Kiyi, let's get down to it. I haven't got long! (*Showing off.*) Excuse us. Brother teaches me to read. See, I ain't one of those ignorant niggers –

Brother Kiyi (*interrupts, re niggers*)   Carl!

Carl   Sorry, Nubians, that afraid of edumacation.

Alice   I see.

Alice *moves to the back of the shop. Puts her headphones back on as politely as possible.* **Carl** *points to the box of provisions.*

Carl   Oh, by the way, that's five sweet potatoes, two giant-sized yams, a bag of rice, and four plantains and a boiler chicken.

Brother Kiyi (*hushed tones*)   I didn't give you money for all of this?

Carl   Well, I told Mr Dongal that you got the eviction letter the other day . . .

Brother Kiyi   You did what? . . .

Carl   . . . and having spent all your money on books nobody's gonna read. Well! So he and some of the other shop-owners clubbed together and sent you this. It's a peace offering.

Brother Kiyi   I was not paying my rent because I object to being bullied by a man who's only been in the country for six months.

Carl   Sure! They're gonna do this every week till you put on some weight.

Brother Kiyi   Are you crazy? Tell them thank you very much, but I don't accept gifts from traitors.

Carl   Don't be like that, Brother Kiyi. The people are showing you that they care . . .

Brother Kiyi   They could have showed that by . . .

Carl   This was my idea, Brother Kiyi, my idea, and for once people listened to me and thought that it was good. Now you are throwing it back in my face!

Brother Kiyi (*conceding*)   OK. Thank you for the gift, Carl. I'll take the food home and give thanks for it.

Carl   Good. Good.

Brother Kiyi *pulls out a book from beneath his counter.*

Brother Kiyi   Alright, where were we? Tell you what, try this today. You may struggle a little but, well . . .

He goes to the shelf and pulls down a selection of poems. He finds one poem and hands the book to **Carl**.

Carl   What is it?

Brother Kiyi   Just read.

Carl   'If we must die.'
    'If we must die, let it not be like hogs
    Hunted and penned in an ingl −'

Brother Kiyi   Inglor −

Carl
                                    '− 'rious spot,
    While round us bark the mad and hungry dogs . . .'

(*Stops reading.*) What does that 'inglorious' mean?

Brother Kiyi   I'll explain after. Carry on.

Carl
    'Making their mock at our ac-curs-èd lot.'

He exhales.

Brother Kiyi   Well done.

Carl
    'If we must die, O let us nobly die,
    So that our precious −'

(*Pleased with himself for recognising.*) That's that word from *Lord of the Rings*, innit? (*Does impression. To* **Alice**.) 'My precious.'

You know, there's an actor from *The Bill* who lives right up the road dere, Brian something or other, he knows the guy that played Golom, you know?

Brother Kiyi   I see. Carry on with the poem, Carl.

Brother Kiyi *is slowly pacing about the shop. He is touching his hair – not something we have seen him do before.*

Carl
> 'Blood may not be shed
> In vain; then even the monsters we defy
> Shall be –'

Brother Kiyi   Constrained . . .

Carl
> '– constrained to honour us, though dead!'

Brother Kiyi   Carry on, Carl.

Carl (*looks at* **Alice**)
> 'O, kinsmen! we must meet the common foe!
> Though far outnumbered let us show us brave,
> And for their thousand blows deal one death-blow!
> What though before us lies the open grave?'

Enter **Kwesi** *from upstairs, who has heard the last few lines. He laughs aloud at* **Carl**'*s reading. He clocks* **Alice** *and likes what he sees but does not show it, much.*

Brother Kiyi *gives* **Kwesi** *a dirty look.* **Kwesi**, *squeezing past* **Alice**, *goes to the back of the shop.*

Alice   Who was that?

Brother Kiyi   Claude McKay.

Carl'*s mobile rings. It's the theme tune to* Batman. **Carl** *looks at the number and recognises it.*

Carl (*sudden remembrance*)   Oh my gosh, Brother Kiyi, I gotta run, Mister Dongal done waiting for me. I liked that poem dough. Explain it to me tomorrow?

Brother Kiyi   Tomorrow!

As he walks past **Alice**, *he smiles.*

Carl (*as he exits, about* **Alice**, *malapropism of course*)   Inglorious!

Brother Kiyi *goes back to his box. After a beat or so* **Alice** *walks towards him.*

Alice (*well reluctant*)   That's very good.

Brother Kiyi   What?

Alice   What you do. Reading and that.

Brother Kiyi   Care of the community! That is what they meant, wasn't it?

Alice   *In* the commu – Speaking of care, Brother Kiyi, I came in today because I wanted to challenge the way you treated me yesterday. Like a common criminal. At least, that's how I felt, and I wanted to let you know that in fact I am a teacher of much repute. I am a woman that should be respected.

Brother Kiyi   I have no doubts that you are. I apologised yesterday, and I will do so again if you wish.

Alice   You didn't, actually.

Brother Kiyi   Didn't what?

Alice   You didn't apologise.

Brother Kiyi   I distinctly remember saying, 'I'm sorry, but one cannot be too careful.'

Alice   Not to split hairs, but that was apologising for having to do it, it wasn't an apology to me.

Brother Kiyi (*laughs*)   What today is? Break-me-balls day?

Alice   Sorry?

Brother Kiyi   What is it you want, young lady? I'm very busy.

Alice   For a start, don't you think if you are introducing him to poetry, which I do think is great, maybe you should choose a less sexist poet?

Brother Kiyi   Less what?

Alice   A poet that doesn't exclude women from participating in 'the struggle', as it were.

Brother Kiyi   It is Claude – the father of the Harlem renaissance, the poet quoted by Winston Churchill to the British soldiers before the Battle of Britain – McKay we are taking about here, isn't it?

Alice   Is it because I'm a woman you use that condescending tone with me?

Brother Kiyi   I'm not using a condescending tone with you.

Alice   Yes, you are! You're talking to me like I'm some 'stupid girl' that doesn't know what she's talking about . . .

Brother Kiyi   Well, I don't think you do actually . . .

Alice   Well, I beg to differ . . .

Brother Kiyi (*confused*)   Young lady, you are unknown to me. Why are you raising your voice?

She pauses for a second and gathers herself.

Alice   I tend to get passionate about what goes into the minds of those we are responsible for. I'm sorry.

Beat.

Brother Kiyi   OK, please explain why Claude McKay is a sexist?

Alice   I didn't actually mean he was sexist, I meant the poem has sexist overtones.

Brother Kiyi   Lord have mercy!

Alice (*reciting as if having just read it*)   The phrase, 'If we must die' utters the poem's call to participation, and it gathers meaning through its repetition in the first and second quatrains . . .

Brother Kiyi   Right . . .

Alice   The phrase 'O kinsmen!' makes that call to participation explicit; the poem's would-be warriors are men. McKay fails to explicate the unique position of women within the embattled Black community, choosing instead to talk about the race by imagining the aspirations of black men.

Brother Kiyi   Rasclaat! I know that essay!

Alice   No, not rasclaat, or however you pronounce it, the contest for black humanity in the poem is waged exclusively through the battle for black masculinity.

Kwesi *enters.*

Kwesi   Yes, it is.

Alice *turns and looks at* **Kwesi**.

Alice *(smiles)*   Exactly.

Kwesi   And what's wrong with that?

Alice *(loses smile)*   Sorry?

Kwesi   What's wrong with that assertion? Battles are fought by men. Not women, not girls, but men.

Alice   I think you'll find that if you look at the number of active servicepeople in the Gulf Wars, Kosovo, Afghanistan, you'll see that the number of women . . .

Kwesi   Is vastly below the number of men. You guys can't have it both ways, you know?

Alice   What guys are we talking about here?

Kwesi   Women! One minute you're the saviour of mankind due to the size of your humanity and now you're the sword-bearers that defend the nation? Which way do you want it?

Alice *(taken aback)*   Wow. I don't know you, sir, but I would say that's a rather archaic viewpoint for such a – *(Chooses her words carefully.)* – modern-looking man.

Kwesi   Books and covers.

Alice   Evidently!

He exits upstairs. There's a moment's silence. **Alice** *switches.*

Alice (*excited*)   What a great place. How many bookstores can you go into and have heated debates like that?

Brother Kiyi   That was my dream.

Alice   Who is that guy?

Brother Kiyi   Kwesi, my militant-in-residence. Head of All-Black-African Party. They meet in the room upstairs. (*Suddenly becoming suspicious.*) Why?

Alice   No reason. (*With passion.*) What a hateful man. That's why people don't go out with black men, you know! (*She stops herself.*)

Pause. She begins to look around the store.

Alice   I finished *The Philosophies of Marcus Garvey* last night.

Brother Kiyi   You did?

Alice   Yes.

Brother Kiyi   What about the other one?

Alice   No, I haven't starting reading that.

Brother Kiyi   Why?

Alice   I kind of wanted to discuss the *Philosophies* book with someone first.

Brother Kiyi   I see.

Alice   But I don't really know anyone that is familiar with the works of Marcus Garvey.

Brother Kiyi   Right.

Alice   I mean, don't you think he's a little racist?

Brother Kiyi   Here we go again!

Alice   No, I mean he comes over to me as a, yeah, a black racist.

Brother Kiyi   You're a teacher, you say?

Alice   Yes, I am?

Brother Kiyi   What do you teach?

Alice   English and – and History.

Brother Kiyi   Just over there you'll find a dictionary, could you pass it to me please.

Alice *does so.*

Brother Kiyi *(slightly exhausted by this)*   Racist, what does it say here in this *Oxford Dictionary*. 'Racism – a feeling of superiority from one race to another.' Now I would argue, not today because I'm tired, that since we are certainly not economically superior, and I would say due to the collective lack of knowledge of ourselves and our constant desire to imitate, impersonate, and duplicate everything Caucasian, à la Michael Jackson, or should I say Michael X, we are neither in a psychological position of superiority. Hence by that definition we cannot be racist.

Alice *(with real concern)*   Why are you tired?

Brother Kiyi *(unsure how to respond)*   I'm fine.

She sits close.

Alice   Like what?

Brother Kiyi *shuts down and starts to read.*

Alice   I've taken six months off work, you know. *(Struggles slightly.)* To – find myself. 'Cos I'm brown, everybody expects me to somehow know everything black. And I'm like, 'Hey, how am I supposed to know what . . . bomboclaat means, I'm from Somerset.'

Brother Kiyi *(now understanding)*   OK!

Alice   People down here are so fortunate to have a resource like this.

Brother Kiyi   You don't miss the water till the well . . .

The phone rings.

Tende Mwari . . . Yes, Brother Peter . . . I see. Have you
spoken to our beloved local MP? . . . Wait a second, I have
his surgery days here . . . Yes . . . Monday at the Town
Hall, Martin Luther King Room, and then Saturday
morning at the Steve Biko Library . . . No, you just turn up
and wait and he'll see you. If you'd like, I have a book here
somewhere on the working of . . . Yes, yes I do. It will
inform you of all, well, most of your rights! . . . Send your
son to pick it up. Four o'clock? . . . Yes, I'll be here . . .
Good luck.

Brother Kiyi *puts down the phone and gets up to search for the*
book. He has to squeeze past **Alice** *to get there.*

Brother Kiyi   Excuse me.

Alice *is quite taken by the smell of his locks.*

Alice   What do you put in your hair?

Brother Kiyi (*sarcastic*)   Um, Oil of Ulay.

Beat.

Alice (*picking up on tone*)   Do you do that for everyone?

Brother Kiyi   What?

Alice   Advise them and then bam, sell 'em a book?

Brother Kiyi   I don't sell the books. I loan them.

Alice   Loan them? Do you get them back? . . .

Brother Kiyi   Most times . . .

Alice   In sellable condition? . . .

Brother Kiyi   Sometimes . . .

Beat.

Alice   How many books do you sell a week?

Brother Kiyi (*a little defensive*)   Why do you ask?

Alice   Curious?

Brother Kiyi   Ah, here it is! (*He takes the book and heads back to his enclosure to wrap it up.*)

Alice   How many books did you loan last week?

Brother Kiyi   About twelve.

Alice   Any come back?

Brother Kiyi   They will.

Alice   You have a record of the books you loaned out, right?

Brother Kiyi (*annoyed*)   What is the problem here? I loan books. If I didn't they wouldn't be read.

Alice   What do you mean by that?

Brother Kiyi   I mean . . . (*Decides to share.*) You know what my best-seller has been for the last year? Apart from my Afrocentric cards, that is – you know: black mum kissing black dad, West Indian grandmother in big hat playing with a cat – um, the best-seller was *Black Love*, and, oh, *Shotter's Revenge*.

Alice   What's wrong with that? I mean I could do with a little black love right now, I tell ya!

He pauses for a millisecond to take that in.

Brother Kiyi   What is wrong with that? I have on these shelves Van Sertima's *Africa, Cradle of Civilisation*! Chancellor Williams' *Destruction of Black Civilisation*, Peterson's *The Middle Passage*, Williams' *Capitalism and Slavery*. I've books on the Dogons, the Ashantis, the – the pyramids of Ancient Zimbabwe, and what do they buy? Nonsensical nonsense about men with nine-packs doing in the sauna with black female executives. What is that, I ask you?

Alice   Six-packs!

Brother Kiyi   What?

Alice   No one has a nine-pack.

Brother Kiyi (*hardcore West Indian*)   I don't care what pack
them have! That is nonsense reading when we face the
things we face today. You know, you were the first person in
a age to buy, well, to buy a book of substance. In fact . . .
(*He runs to his book of sales and looks it up.*) Yes, here it is!
December of last year. One copy of *The Isis Papers* by Dr
Cress Welsing. And that customer wasn't even black!

Alice   She was white?

Brother Kiyi   No, she was mixed. (*He stops himself.*)

Alice   I believe the term is now person of dual heritage.

Brother Kiyi   I'm sure it is.

Alice   Shouldn't you be up-to-date on that sort of stuff?
Being a leader of your community an' all?

Brother Kiyi   I suppose I should, if in fact I were a leader.

Alice   Why aren't you?

Brother Kiyi   A leader or up-to-date?

Alice   Both.

Brother Kiyi   You ask a lot of questions?

Alice   I need a lot of answers. Always have.

Brother Kiyi   Answers to what? You a policewoman?

Alice   No I am not. . . . Denied histories are fascinating
to me.

Brother Kiyi   I wish that more of my community thought
like that.

Alice (*little side*)   Maybe they do and just haven't told you.

Brother Kiyi   They'd tell me alright, but only after the
white man gives his seal of approval. Mek the BBC do a
series about when them deliberately infect three hundred
African-Americans with syphilis in the thirties, and watch, the
next day, ten man will run in here and say, 'Kiyi, you see

that programme last night about the VD dem give dem man
dem? Woooo, me never know that.' But I've been telling
them for years. There's fifteen different books on my shelves
written by esteemed black scholars, but when I tell you, no!
It's Black Power fantasy, but mek the white man tell you
that just before *Eastenders* and, Lord have mercy, it must be
true! Mek a news item run saying that a great resource might
soon be lost to the community and hey presto, X-amount of
gravy-train Negroes that never come in here in they life go
on TV as cultural commentators. Everybody will claim to
have bought a book from here. They'll all come running in.
Why? Because the white man say so. But hey! That's just my
opinion.

Alice   So are you about to close down?

Brother Kiyi   No! I'm gearing up for round two!

Alice   I know this friend of mine, I mean he's white, but
really deep in his heart he's . . . well. He works for the
BBC. I'm sure he'd be very interested in doing something
about, you know, your shop, the plight!

Brother Kiyi (*vexed*)   Thank you, but no.

Alice   What is your problem with white?

He suddenly remembers and stands.

Brother Kiyi   Sugar, what time is it now?

Alice   Have I kept you?

He runs to the back.

Brother Kiyi   Kwesi! Kwesi!

Kwesi (*off*)   Yo!

Brother Kiyi   Come and hold the store for me, please.
Got to run out the road.

Kwesi (*off*)   I'll be down in second.

Brother Kiyi   I've got to go now!

Kwesi (*off*)   OK, go, I'll be down in a minute.

Brother Kiyi *grabs his coat and checks that the envelope is secure and heads to the door.*

Brother Kiyi   You don't have to leave now, you can, you know, look around still? There's a chair there.

She runs up to him and hugs him passionately – almost girl-like, but she's a woman. **Brother Kiyi** *doesn't quite know how to deal with that much affection.*

Brother Kiyi (*shouts up the stairs*)   Kwesi! Kwesi!

Brother Kiyi *strokes his hair. Then exits.*

When it's clear he's gone, as if she has been holding her breath for an hour, almost as if she is hyperventilating, **Alice** *begins to exhale loudly. She takes a little while to gather herself.*

Alice *walks around the shop, looking at things more freely now that she is by herself. She sees the slave narratives. At first she about to take down the book named –*

Alice   Slave Auctions. (*But decides to read the book called* Family.) No, I think you'll be the one, thank you. (*She goes into the box and looks around. She looks though the contents of the desk, and then under the counter. She stays there for a little while.*) Bloody hell, this man's organised. Magazine articles by prominent black thinkers in alphabetical order.

She discovers and pulls up the old thick box that Brother Kiyi placed there earlier. She puts it on the table. However, it's locked. She can't resist it. She attempts to undo the lock. It doesn't give. She tries to prise it open, then decides against it. She places it back. Slightly disappointed.

She makes herself comfortable. She begins to read. The lights lower to a spotlight on her. We are in her head. She takes on the voice of the storyteller.

Alice   'Mary Gould, Grand Anse Estate, Grenada. One day Masser Reynolds come back from Barbados wid one high yellow gal he just buy. They say she was real pretty but

I can hardly remember. But he never put she to live wid the other niggers, no, he buil' she a special little house away from the qua'ters down by the river which run at the back ah de plantation. Every negroes know Masser take a black woman quick as he did a white and took any on his place that he wanted and he took them often. But most his pickney dem born on the place looked like niggers. But not all. Once, two ah dem went up to the big house where Dr Reynolds' child dem was playing in their dolls' house and told them that they want to play in the dolls' house too. The story go that one of the Doctor full-breed child say, "Sorry this is for white children only." The reply I'm told went, "We ain't no niggers, 'cos we got the same daddy you has, and he comes to see us every day with gifts and wonderful clothes and such." Well, of course Mrs Reynolds who was at the window heard the white niggers saying, "He is our daddy 'cos we call him Daddy when he comes to see our mammy." That evening I get whipped for almost three hours. And within one year all my children had been sold away from me. (**Alice** *repeats for clarity.*) Within one year all my children had been sold away from me. No sir, it don't pay to be pretty and yella'.'

*The lights snap on as **Kwesi** rests his hands on **Alice**'s shoulders. She jumps.*

Alice   Ohhhh.

Kwesi   Did I scare you?

Alice   Yes, you did actually. What are you doing over my shoulder?

Kwesi   You were breathing heavily.

Alice   I was reading!

Kwesi   Do you always breathe like that when you read?

Alice   I mouth the words as well!

Kwesi   You into that stuff?

Alice   Families?

Kwesi   Slavery! Old Kiyi here is addicted to that shit.

Alice   Aren't all you political types?

Kwesi   Hell, no. I only look forward, sister.

Alice   So your march about being paid back for slavery
is . . . ?

Kwesi   . . . about the future!

Alice   Sounds rather disrespectful of Brother Kiyi!

Kwesi   No, it's not. He's cool. Big expert on all things
slavery. Which is good for me 'cos I don't have to go to no
Yanks when I wanna know something. I hate going to those
Yanks. Been in the belly of the beast too long.

Alice   What does that mean?

Kwesi   It affects you, you know? Being around too much
white folk. I seen the bluest of blackest men get too much
exposure, bam, they lose their rhythm. Put on a James
Brown tune and they start doing the Charleston to Ras!

Alice (acidic)   Isn't there an ointment you can get to
mitigate against that?

Kwesi   What?

Alice - Over-exposure to white folk?!

Kwesi   Ohhhh, somebody's getting touchy!

Alice   I'm not getting touchy.

Kwesi   Yes, you are. I say the word white folk and you get
all arms!

Alice   Two words, actually. Arms?

Kwesi   Vex! Wanna fight!

Alice   I don't want to fight you!

Kwesi   Why not? It's half your people, innit, that I'm
cussing, innit?!

She pauses to gather herself.

Alice (*realises*)   Half my p – ? You're trying to provoke me. Why?

Kwesi   You look like the type that likes to be provoked,

Alice   Well, Mr Kwesa –

Kwesi   Kwesi, Kwes-i, not ah.

Alice   Sorry. It doesn't exactly roll off my half-tongue.

Kwesi   Very good. If you were 'fuller' I could quite like you.

Alice   Is that of body or of race?

Kwesi   Ummm, both.

Alice (*takes the front foot*)   If you're gonna come on to me, at least engage on a higher level than that?

Kwesi (*slightly taken aback*)   I wasn't trying to come on to you.

Alice   Is that so?

Kwesi   I don't do your type!

Alice   My . . . And what is my type exactly?

Kwesi   West Indians. You guys are weak.

Alice   Yanks, West Indians, mixed. And there was I thinking it was because I'm from Somerset.

Kwesi   You're funny. I like you.

Alice   All of me or half?

Kwesi   Depends what side of you you're showing me?

Alice *shakes her head.*

Kwesi   Let me come straight, Alice. I don't trust you. Who are you and what are you doing here?

Alice   What is it to you who I am?

Kwesi   Nothing. Like I said, I just don't trust you.

Alice   Well, it's a good thing I'm not here for you, then.

There's a shout from upstairs: 'Kwesi!' Beat.

Kwesi   Know that I'm watching you, child. I'm coming!

He exits up the stairs. As he is walking, she clocks his arse. He turns but doesn't see her do that. She sits in the chair and begins to read.

Lights down.

Scene Three

Fix Up Bookstore. Day.

While the lights are down, we hear playing quietly in the background **Brother Kiyi***'s favourite recording, from 1963, of James Baldwin being interviewed by the academic Kenneth Clark.*

Voice of Baldwin   Now, we all knew. I know you knew, and I knew, too, that a moment was coming when we couldn't guarantee, that no one can guarantee, that we won't reach the breaking point, you know? You can only survive so many beatings, so much humiliation, so much despair, so many broken promises, before something gives. Human beings are not by nature non-violent.

Voice of Clark   So you are pessimistic about the future of this country?

Voice of Baldwin   To be a pessimist means that you have agreed that human life is an academic matter, so I'm forced to be an optimist. I'm forced to believe that we can survive whatever we must survive. But the future of the Negro in this country is precisely as bright or as dark as the future of the country. It is entirely up to the American people and our representatives – it is entirely up to the American people whether or not they are going to face, and deal with, and embrace this stranger whom they maligned so long.

Lights up.

Brother Kiyi　Speak, Brother James, speak! Shit, you make me happy!

Brother Kiyi *is in joyous mood. He runs over to the cassette recorder and throws in another cassette. It throws out a very percussive rhythm made up of hand-claps and foot-stomps.* **Brother Kiyi** *starts to sing an old slave work chant. It's a call and response.* **Brother Kiyi** *is calling, the recording responding. The lead line sounds like a blues refrain. He begins to dance with it, as if he is picking cotton from the ground and then cutting cane with two cutlasses.*

Brother Kiyi　Ohhh, Eve, where is Adam?

Response　Picking up leaves.

Brother Kiyi　Oh oh, Adam?

Response　Picking up leaves.

Brother Kiyi　Why don't you answer?

Response　Picking up leaves.

Brother Kiyi　Oh Adam?

Response　Picking up leaves.

Brother Kiyi　Why don't you answer?

Response　Picking up leaves.

Brother Kiyi　Why's God calling?

Response　Do you believe?

Brother Kiyi　Eve and Adam.

Response　Don't you believe?

Brother Kiyi　Adam won't answer.

Response　Picking up leaves.

Brother Kiyi　Who told you, Adam?

Response　Picking up leaves.

Brother Kiyi   That you would make it?

Response   Picking up leaves.

Brother Kiyi   Ohhhh Adammm!

Response   Picking up leaves.

Brother Kiyi   Oh Adammmmm!

Enter **Norma**. **Brother Kiyi** *stops dancing for a moment, then continues.*

Norma   Boy, what you so happy about?

Brother Kiyi   You like the rhythm, gal?

Norma   I would if it wasn't so blasted loud!

Brother Kiyi   What you say?

Norma   Turn that blasted ting down.

He does.

Brother Kiyi   You becoming like dem English people, you know. 'Fraid a noise! The girl that live in the flat above me, soon as she next-door neighbour start to play he music, not even loud you know, she down knocking the door, knocking the door . . .

Norma   I've heard your 'not even loud' . . .

Brother Kiyi   Char! Telling him, in she condescending tone, how she go call the noise police. Noise police! You see that is advance citizenship for you. In most countries you have police to keep the people under manners. Here you have a force to discipline a bass line! What a topsy-turvy Babylonian system.

Norma   That must fall down.

Brother Kiyi   That must fall down . . .

Gets out draughts board.

Norma   Don't watch Babylon, you give the man he money?

Brother Kiyi   When I hand it him, he shit! All he could do was open he mouth so. (*Imitates jaw dropping.*) You know who was in the office? The same boys he selling it to. Oh God, it was sweet. Thank you, gal.

Norma   (*smiles*) Good.

They sit down to play. He suddenly catches sight of her hair. She is wearing a very long and glamorous wig. It stops just beneath her shoulders.

Brother Kiyi   What, gal! A next animal ting you have on you head. It still alive?

Norma   Don't be feisty. It's one-hundred-per-cent human!

Brother Kiyi   Human?

Norma   Yes.

Brother Kiyi   As oppose to what?

Norma   Horse!

She gets the draughts.

Brother Kiyi   So you will spend your hard-earned money on hair dem chop from a horse?

Norma   I told you it's not no horse hair, it's one-hundred-per-cent Chinese.

Brother Kiyi   Chinese?

Norma   (*stops him*) Kiyi! Make we concentrate on the game?

He makes a move.

Norma   Kiyi, you does need any special qualification to go into politics?

Brother Kiyi   Apart from a great capacity for wickedness, no. Why?

Norma   I went to the meeting at the Town Hall last night, and when me stand up you know how they introduce me?

'Madam Norma, a woman who knows this community like no other.' You know how great that mek me feel? The head of the council calling me 'madam'! The only time I get call 'madam' previous to dat in me life is when they come to me house to arrest me first-born.

Brother Kiyi What dat have to do wid your Chinese wig, Norma?

Norma If you gonna stand for election you have to look glamorous, don't it?

Brother Kiyi Election of what?

Norma I don't know, I'm not too stupid to run for local councillor or something.

Brother Kiyi Norma, you don't even like politics?

Norma I don't understand it, Kiyi! But before me dead, I'd like to understand something, something from the inside. That's why me and you generation fail, boy. We didn't engage. You can't fight from the outside alone. I mean, look at you! How long you going to carry on so? No customers, no life . . .

Brother Kiyi Norma, I told you it's not going to stay so! Na man, I can smell it in the air. (*Beat.*) You see that young girl that does come in here, right . . .

Norma . . . the half-caste gal . . .?

Brother Kiyi Woman of dual heritage! Comes in here every day! Different dread. Angry, political, albeit about woman tings, but still fantastic anger. I does sit down and talk to that girl and I does say to meself, wooooy, where does that rage come from in these apathetic times? Then the wind whisper in me ears, 'Ah, my time again.' That's why I know it's coming.

Ting. Enter **Alice**. *They turn round and look at her.*

Alice What?

Brother Kiyi   Nothing. Talking about you, not to you, hahaha.

Norma *looks at him.*

Brother Kiyi   Right!

The women look at each other.

Norma (*to* **Brother Kiyi**, *looking at his crotch*)   You sure it's the wind?

Brother Kiyi   Norma! Those new book by S. Pearl Harris come in, you know. They're over there.

Brother Kiyi *points to the back of the shop, and* **Norma** *moves away.*

Alice   How are you today?

Brother Kiyi   Good. Very good. You?

Alice   Oh, OK! I got a call from my boyfriend this morning!

Brother Kiyi's *heart sinks, but he doesn't let it show.*

Brother Kiyi   Boyfriend?

Alice   Well, ex.

Brother Kiyi   What did he want?

Alice   He wanted me to come back to him.

Brother Kiyi   Do you want to?

Alice   He's no good for me. It's time I either had wild abandoned sex with whoever I want, whenever I want, or settled down to have a family.

Brother Kiyi   Can't you do both with him?

Alice   He's married. In fact, his daughter and I are roughly the same age. I know what you're thinking . . .

Brother Kiyi   I don't think you do!

Alice   I mean, guys my age are great for sex and that but, well . . . I need more. I love him, but, ahhh I'm confused. I don't know what to think.

Brother Kiyi *doesn't quite know how to respond.*

Alice   My father always used to warn me, 'What men say and what they really mean are often two different things.' If I were your child, what would you tell me to do?

Brother Kiyi   Stick with the older man. Only joking . . .

Enter **Carl** *in a rush.*

Carl   Brother Kiyi, Brother Kiyi. What's up wid your phone, man?

Brother Kiyi *quickly picks it up. It's dead. He doesn't answer.*

Brother Kiyi   Calm down. What's the matter, Carl?

Carl   Della's been trying to get hold of you! She needs you to go to see her. Good ting I was passing with Dongol!

Brother Kiyi   See me for what?

Carl   She's gonna tell me that, innit? But her face looked dread! Dongol said it's because Mustaphar's about to . . .

Brother Kiyi   Alright, alright. Come and sit the shop for me. (*To* **Alice**.) Excuse me a moment, yeah?

Alice   Of course. Are you OK?

Brother Kiyi   Some people feel they playing with a boy! Well, they go see. Yes, it's all fine. Little while, yeah?

Carl   Yeah. Everything's safe wid me!

Brother Kiyi *pauses and looks at* **Carl** *for a beat before leaving.* **Carl** *stands a fair distance from* **Alice**. *He's kinda smiling at her.*

Carl   Oh well.

Alice   What?

Carl   Nothing. Just oh well! Here we are. The two of us.

Alice   Is – is Kiyi going to be OK?

Carl   Ah yeah, man, he's used to fighting. You don't see the locks? Lion of Judah! . . . They ain't taking nothing from him, dread. This place is too good for anyone to take away. It's great here, don't you think?

Alice   Suppose I do.

Carl   It's a real tribute to Kiyi. Different people coming and going. I mean look at you. You've come in an' caught the bug, right, like the rest of us?

Alice   What bug is that?

Carl   Culture. Nothing like knowing your roots! (*He starts to reggae DJ.*)

Me love me roots and culture, murderer.
How black people dem a suffer – murderer!

Alice *looks on bemused.*

Carl (*a little embarrassed*)   Oh. it's an old Shabba Ranks tune. It must be great being you.

Alice   Wow, where did that come from?

Carl   Yeah, you like must have the best of two worlds, innit? Like you got the black-beauty bit and you got the white-money bit. Hoorah!

Alice   Hoorah!

Carl (*upbeat*)   Roots, you know, connection! I use to want to be white till I met Kiyi. Now I'm blue black brother. You couldn't make me white if you tried!

Alice   You think people try?

Carl   People try anything in this day and age, you know! Is your hair easy to maintain?

Alice   Um, yes, I suppose.

Carl   Though I don't wanna be white, that's what I'd like. The mixed flowy type of hair. Girls like that, don't they? It's so beautiful.

Alice   I think your hair is fine.

Carl   You're just saying to sweet me. You don't have to do that!

Alice *smiles.*

Carl   Look, I'm gonna go do some reading. So, um, feel free to do what you want. Sure Kiyi wont mind.

Alice   Yeah, Kiyi said it OK.

Carl   Good.

He moves across to the desk and takes out a book.

Carl (*sings to himself*)
    'From the very first time I set my eyes on you,
    Girl, my heart said follow though,
    But I know that I'm way down on your line.
    But the waiting deal is fine.'

Enter **Kwesi**. *He clocks* **Alice**.

Kwesi   You still here, girl?

Alice   (*getting up*) See you later, Carl.

Alice *leaves.* **Carl** *walks up to* **Kwesi** *and attempts to take the box from him.*

Carl   Why you always got to be troubling people, Kwesi?

Kwesi   You got to lean on people sometimes to know who they are.

Carl   She's pretty, innit?

Kwesi   She alright. (*Re box.*) No, it's alright.

Carl   Hey, my job is delivery, that's what I do! (*He pulls the box.*)

Kwesi   Carl, I said it's OK.

Carl   Let me take the box. Your car's gonna get a ticket.

Kwesi   I said it's alright.

In a sudden burst of temper **Carl** *pushes the box out of* **Kwesi**'s *hands.*

Carl   Keep your fucking boxes, then!

Kwesi   What the fuck!

Carl (*immediately retracts*)   Sorry.

It falls on the floor and bursts open. Lots of hair products spill onto the floor.

Kwesi   Are you losing your blasted mind?

Carl (*spits it out*)   I just like things to be clear, you know what I am saying? Know what I'm doing, know where I am?

Kwesi *tries to get the stuff back into the box as quickly as possible.* **Carl** *gets down to help him. He notices the hair products.*

Kwesi   Get off.

Carl   Sorry, sorry. (*He picks up a bottle.*) Oh shit, I haven't seen one of these in ages. Gerry Curl Max. (*Fake-sprays it on his hair. Advert voice.*) 'Makes your hair wavyyyy.'

Kwesi   Put that down! Give it to me!

Carl   What you doing with hair products, Kwesi? You boys don't like that shit? (*Impersonates.*) 'Making your hair like white folk!'

Kwesi   Don't worry about that. Just shut you mouth. You get me?

Carl   Just looking forward to seeing you with a perm! It's gonna suit you, trust me!

Kwesi *kisses his teeth and exits.* **Carl** *sits down.*

Lights down.

Scene Four

Fix Up Bookstore. Day.

Lights come up slowly. Enter **Brother Kiyi** *through the front door as slowly as the fade. He walks up to the stairs and shouts.*

Brother Kiyi   Hello!

No one replies. He goes into his enclosure and pops in his Marcus Garvey cassette. It is the same hissy one we heard at the start, with Marcus foot-down-to-the-ground on passionate. **Brother Kiyi** *has a bunch of job adverts in his hands. He is screwing them up and throwing them into the donations bin.*

Brother Kiyi   Cleaning staff, no . . . IT, no . . . Warehouse staff. Another no! No, no, no!

Brother Kiyi *locks the door and turns the volume up on the cassette.*

Voice of Marcus   Our critics said the race problem would be solved through higher education. Through better education that black and white will come together, that day will never happen until Africa is redeemed! Those, like W. E. Dubois who believe that the race problem in America will be solved by higher education will walk between now and eternity and never see the problem solved. (*Applause.*)

Walking back he stops. Standing in the middle of the shop is **Brother Kiyi**. *It is like he is listening to his favourite song, like he's being fed from above by its vibrations.*

Brother Kiyi   Preach, Marcus, preach!

Voice of Marcus   God made man lord of his creation, gave him possession and ownership of the world and you have been so damned lazy that you've allowed the other fella to run away with the whole world and now he's bluffing you and telling you that the world belongs to him and you play no part in it!

Brother Kiyi   Yes, yes!

Voice of Marcus   If black people knew their glorious past they would be more inclined to respect themselves.

As he proclaims his 'Yes!' **Brother Kiyi** *begins to sob, silently at first. Eventually he bends over with the pain. Slowly and quietly we hear his sobs.*

After a beat or two, he inhales and then forcefully exhales the air to pull himself together. He returns to the box, switches off the cassette, goes to the front door of the shop and unlocks it. He returns to his box, looks beneath his desk and pulls out the old-looking box. He takes a key that he has on a chain around his neck and unlocks the box, removing the photo album that is inside. He stares at the first few pictures before drifting off into a state of great sadness.

Brother Kiyi   I don't done pay yet, girl? I've given back! What I go do now? (*He sits there staring into the thin air.*)

Enter **Carl**.

Carl   Hey, Brother Kiyi, you OK?

Brother Kiyi   Yeah, man, course I'm OK.

Carl   How did the Della meeting go?

Brother Kiyi   Fine, fine. She just wanted to talk to me about future plans and tings.

Carl   Tings?

Brother Kiyi   You know, expansion.

Carl   Right. (*Clocks the papers.*) So the shop's cool?

Brother Kiyi   Yeah, man. Safe as it's ever been.

Carl   Seen. Wanna cup of tea or something?

Brother Kiyi   No.

Beat.

Carl   Here what! I wanna do something right, and I think you'd like it too. It's old-skool African.

Brother Kiyi   Alright.

Carl   I wanna ask Alice to marry me and if she says yes, I wanna do right here, in this shop.

Brother Kiyi   Marry you?

Carl   Yes! Will you give me away?

Brother Kiyi   What?

Carl   Best man then, whatever! Truth is, you been like a dad to me. Plus I ain't got no mates. But that's wholly secondary.

Brother Kiyi (*stunned*)   Carl . . . have I missed . . . have you and Alice had anything?

Carl   Not really! . . .

Brother Kiyi   . . . Then you don't know if she feels anything for you, and you want to propose?

Carl   I know she feels something for me, Kiyi. I feel it in bloodstream. Shit that powerful don't happen one-way, it just don't . . . So, what's the best way for me to approach this? Bend down on one knee? Send her a letter? I saw that in a movie the other day, *Roxi* or *Roxette* or something. The man was dumb like me, but got his homey to write her a letter and when she got it, mannn, she was over the moon.

Brother Kiyi   Carl, I think it's a bad idea.

Carl   OK, scrap the letter?

Brother Kiyi   Asking Alice to marry you. (*Almost laughing.*) Are you mad?!

Carl (*takes umbrage at 'mad'*)   What did you call me?

Brother Kiyi   I don't mean mad as in madness, I meant, I meant . . .

Carl   Meant what? What you calling me mad for?

Brother Kiyi   I'm not, I'm simply saying . . . maybe you've misread . . .

Carl   I can't misread what's in my heart, Kiyi!

Brother Kiyi I can't doubt that you feel as if you love
her –

Carl I don't feel, I know!

Brother Kiyi   – but before you run off proposing to any
woman, you got to make sure that it is something they
would like, that you're compatible, that . . .

Carl Oh, I see where you're going now! You think that
I'm not good enough for her?

Brother Kiyi I never said that, Carl.

Carl (*begins to get irate*) Yes you did. You said 'compatible'.
What does that mean? It means that you think she couldn't
love a something like me . . . what, what? Am I too dark for
her or something?

Brother Kiyi Oh, Carl, come on. That's not what I
meant!

Carl (*shouts*) Yes it is! I'm alright for all those other girls
round here, but Alice, noooo?!

Brother Kiyi Carl, calm down now. You're gonna start to
hyperventilate.

Carl I don't care!

Brother Kiyi Carl, calm down! Count to ten, come on,
slowly! One . . .

Carl I'm not a crack addict any more, Kiyi, I'm educated,
and I won't be a delivery boy for ever neither. What dem
say? Behind every great man is a great woman, well, I never
had a great woman behind me, Kiyi, and I want it now.

Brother Kiyi Carl . . .

Carl What's wrong with wanting something, eh? I mean,
you're treating me like the enemy and you don't understand,
you ain't looking. Kwesi's getting his business sorted out,
I heard them last night, Norma's got her family, what about
me? What am I going to have?

Brother Kiyi Breathe, please!

Carl If it's because she's mixed . . . My mother used to say that our great-grandfather on her mother's side came from Spain, I got white in me!

Brother Kiyi *gets close to* **Carl**.

Brother Kiyi I know you do . . . That's good; nice and calm.

Carl Then why are you treating me like this? I may have done bad things but I ain't killed anyone!

Beat.

Brother Kiyi That's low. I'm trying to protect you . . .

Carl That's what they used to say in da madhouse before they – (*Slaps his arm as if to show injection.*) – in the courthouse, in my mum's house before she box me in me mouth! . . .

Brother Kiyi Carl, you know how much pain a bad union can bring?

Carl (*walks to the door*) Pain? What you know about pain? Pain is what you just done to me, dread. You hurt me, Kiyi, you done fucked up. Don't worry about it, though.

Brother Kiyi Carl!

Carl *walks out of the door just as* **Alice** *comes in. They nearly collide.*

Alice Hi, Carl . . .

Carl Don't touch me, go away. (*He exits.*)

Beat.

Alice What's the matter with Carl?

Brother Kiyi Nothing. We, um, just had a little . . . you know, families do that, right?

Alice But he's not your family!

Brother Kiyi   Carl is like a son to me. Both of the boys are.

She doesn't reply.

Beat. He feels some vibes coming off her.

Brother Kiyi   Alice, I've had a really hard day, I'm about to lock up.

Alice   I've never seen you upset before. I only came to return this. (*She pulls out a narrative from her bag.*) I borrowed it last night?

Brother Kiyi   You did?

Alice   Didn't think you'd mind, you lend books all of the time, don't you?

Brother Kiyi (*a little annoyed*)   Not those I don't.

Alice   Why not those?

Brother Kiyi   Because they're really not supposed to leave the store. Why would you do that without asking me?

Alice   I'm sorry if I took your book home without permission, but I've never seen, read anything like this before. I couldn't put it down . . .

Brother Kiyi *doesn't answer.*

Alice   I read a story by this woman whose children wanted to play in the dolls' house of their brother and sister and the mother got whipped and her children sold and she kinda looked like me. And . . .

Brother Kiyi   I know the one . . .

Alice   . . . I've found this other story. (*She carefully pulls it out of her bag.*) As I lay on my bed imagining, feeling for these people, I couldn't let go of my stomach. Listen to this!

She sits in exactly the same way that he is seated. She reads to **Brother Kiyi** *quickly.*

Alice   'When me mudder see that Mr Reynolds had really collected me to sell with the other ten or so pickney she fell to her knees and begged him to spare me. When she seed that it weren't no good she simply stood up and asked my master if he would ask whoever it was dat buyed me, to raise me for God. I was too young to understand what was going on, but now I understand. I never seed my modder again all my living days. Rachel Reynolds.' (*Beat.*) I was given away, and I tried to imagine the pain of that mother what that mother felt, that parent felt, but I just simply couldn't.

Brother Kiyi   Given away?

Alice (*didn't mean for that to come out, brushes it off*)   Adopted. Yeah! Can you imagine the pain of that parent?

Brother Kiyi (*thinks*)   No!

Alice   The pain of that child when she realised she would never see her parents again? Can you imagine?

Beat.

Brother Kiyi   Yes, I can. I can because I wrote them.

Alice   Wrote what?

Looks around to see that no one else is in the shop.

Brother Kiyi   I, I, wrote those, what I should say is that I painstakingly, lovingly translated them. I mean hell, if King James can do it?

Alice   Translated what?

Brother Kiyi   The American originals. They're not West Indians at all. But they could be! Alice, for years people come in here and ask for their slave stories, their histories and what do I have give them? Bloody American history. Why should the British, the biggest slavers, get away with it? No!

Alice   So these are not true?

Brother Kiyi   Truth is whatever you choose to believe. (*Pulling back.*) But of course you're right . . . I kinda started one evening at home, it was just an exercise, but I couldn't stop. Before I knew it I was paying the bookbinders, all I have, but look what I got? I have something that I did. Look how you were affected!

Alice   That still doesn't make them the truth. (*She looks at him.*)

Brother Kiyi   I'm not going to sell them. I don't even want them to come out of the store.

Alice   You care that much?

Brother Kiyi   We're the bottom of the tree here, Alice. Every second of everybody else's life is recorded. Every facet covered in films or books or something. What about us? Yes, I do care that much.

He grabs her hands as if trying to convince her.

Beat.

Alice   Are you attracted to me, Kiyi?

Brother Kiyi   In what sense?

Alice   I don't know, just attracted.

Brother Kiyi   I don't think so, no.

Alice (*slightly offended*)   Am I ugly to you?

Brother Kiyi   No, of course not.

Alice   Then what's the problem?

Brother Kiyi   There is no problem. I just meant that at this precise moment when I'm talking about something . . . other . . . it is not something I can think about . . . Why are you testing me?

Alice   I'm not testing, I just, I just feel ugly today and I want to hear that I'm not.

Beat.

Brother Kiyi (*cool at first*)   This shop has been lit up by
your beauty. On Monday, Alice, this will be a centre of
excellence for black hair products. Run by two very nice-
looking Turkish guys. They don't have a great grasp of English
at the moment, but I'm sure they've enough to know the
difference between Afro Sheen and Dyke 'n' Dryden. It's not
a problem, in fact I feel rather good that in the first months
of trading no doubt more black folk will have passed through
here than I'd have seen in my whole fifteen years! What is a
problem is that I must start anew, afresh. Again. I hear you
about feeling ugly.

Alice *doesn't quite know what to say.*

Brother Kiyi   However, today you have added power to
my depleted strength. You're an angel, and I thank you.

Alice *just stares at him. Suddenly she bursts into tears and runs out
of the store.*

Brother Kiyi *doesn't know how to react to this. After a beat or so
he switches into another mode. He rummages underneath the desk. He
pulls out a very sharp-looking knife. He stares at it. He looks round the
store.*

Brother Kiyi (*after a deep breath*)   If it is so, it is so. OK! It's
time to deal with you, Mister!

Lights down.

Scene Five

Fix Up Bookstore. The next day. **Kwesi** *is in the shop alone. He is
looking around as if sizing up the place. There's a knock on the front
door of the store. It's* **Alice**. *She knocks three or four times before*
Kwesi *eventually goes to the door.*

Kwesi   Kiyi's out, you know!

Alice   Cool, I'll wait for him.

Kwesi   He didn't tell me to let anyone in?

Alice   Oh come on, Kwesi, open the door, it's cold out here.

He does.

Kwesi (*without emotion*)   New hairstyle. Nice.

Alice   Thank you for noticing.

Kwesi   Hold the fort, please, not that anyone's coming in here. Any problems, I'm upstairs.

Alice   As usual.

Kwesi   As usual!

Alice   Would be nice sometimes to converse!

Kwesi   Yeah, it would, wouldn't it.

He leaves for upstairs. **Alice** *goes to sit in the enclosure. She looks round, not really knowing what to do.*

Beat, beat, beat.

Suddenly she begins to search for the old box placed beneath Brother Kiyi's desk. At first she can't find it. Then she does. **Alice** *puts the box onto the desk. She begins to try to prise it open with her hands. She sees a letter-opener on the desk. She takes that and attempts to break into the box.*

The box slips and falls to the ground, making a loud noise. She picks it up, after looking to see if Kwesi is coming. She starts again. This time **Alice** *manages to open the box, but not before knocking over the chair.*

She pulls out the old photo album. **Alice** *is a little surprised. She holds it in her hands but doesn't open it for a moment. She checks over her shoulder that no one is around, and nervously places it on the table.*

If we could hear her heart beating it would be dangerously fast.

As she sits, the lights slowly dim until she is in a spotlight. She opens the photo album and turns to the first page. She gasps, covers her mouth with her hand as if trying to keep in what wants to come gushing out, and stares at the picture.

She turns to the next page, and spontaneously tears begin to fall. She quickly turns to the next page, and the next, and lands on one that instantly makes her clench her teeth, cover both her eyes and silently moan.

Suddenly the lights snap back up. A hand lands on her shoulder. She jumps up.

Alice (*shouts*)   Ahhhhh! What the hell are you doing? (*She slams the album shut behind her, almost hiding it.*)

Kwesi   I heard a bang . . .

Alice (*real anger*)   . . . Haven't I told you before about creeping up on me?

Kwesi   I wasn't creeping up on you . . .

Alice   Of course you were . . .

Kwesi   Easy na! Calm down. I wasn't . . .

He makes to touch her. She recoils.

Alice (*barks*)   Don't tell me what to do! . . .

Kwesi   I'm not *telling* you anything . . .

Alice (*screams*)   Yes you *are*!

He attempts to grab her.

Kwesi (*losing his temper*)   Listen . . .

Alice   Get off . . .

She starts to hit him in his chest.

Get off me . . .

He holds her tighter to calm her down.

Kwesi   I don't know about, mans, where you come from, but don't be shouting up at me.

They are face to face.

Alice   Why, what you gonna do, hit me? I'm used to that . . .

Kwesi   Don't be stupid – what am I going to hit you for?

Alice   Then what? What? Whatever you're gonna do, do it!

She begins to sob. **Kwesi** *doesn't know what to do.*

Alice   Jesus! . . .

Kwesi (*confused by this outburst*)   Woo! Ummm . . .

Still in his arms, she turns away.

Alice (*talking to herself*)   I'm strong, pull yourself . . . Come
on . . . Don't be stupid . . . Don't cry, you silly girl . . .

Kwesi *starts to look at the desk. It must be something she was
reading. He sees the photo album.*

Alice   I gotta call home . . . No . . .

Kwesi *lets her go. She instantly moves away as if attempting to
gather her things and run.* **Kwesi** *moves towards the desk. Just as he
is about to open the photo album, she turns and sees him.*

Alice   Nooooo . . .

*He looks up. Thinking quickly, she runs up to him and kisses him
deeply. Unsure of what is going on, he half-kisses her back. She moves
herself between* **Kwesi** *and the album.*

The kissing becomes more intense. **Alice** *starts to undo his shirt. He is
a little surprised but allows her to do it. She takes it off, throws it
away and then begins to undo his trousers.*

Kwesi   What are you? . . .

She puts her finger to his lips.

Alice   Ssssshhhh!

*She starts to kiss him. He takes her by the hand as if to lead her
upstairs. She pulls him back into the enclosure.*

Alice   No. I want you here.

*She starts to kiss him again, almost violently. She then turns round,
lifts up her skirt and places her hands either side of the photo album on
the desk.* **Kwesi** *is unsure.*

Alice *turns round and looks at him. He undoes his flies and takes her from behind. One slam, two, after the third he pulls out.*

Kwesi (*firmly*)   Upstairs.

He takes her by the hand and leads her upstairs. She follows, still staring back at the photo album. As they reach the stairs she kisses him.

Silence.

Then we start to hear the sounds of heavy fucking. Not necessarily vocal but the sound of the room being rocked.

After a few beats **Carl** *enters the shop. He marches to the desk as if about to have it out with Brother Kiyi.*

Carl   Kiyi! Let me tell you . . .

When he gets there he doesn't, of course, see anyone. He looks around. Suddenly he hears the sounds from upstairs. At first he stands still and listens hard to clarify what it is.

Carl   Kiyi?

Then he hears **Alice** *moan.*

Alice (*off*)   Ahhhhh!

Carl *covers his ears instantly, blocking out the sound.*

Carl   Oahh. No. No.

Eventually he takes his hands away but it's still going on. The unmistakable sounds of heavy slamming. Almost laughing, he punches himself on the head.

Carl   Idiot! Idiot! Course you didn't want me to marry her. You wanted to . . . fuck her yourself, didn't you . . . (*The anger rises.*) You fucking – (*He pushes the books off the desk.*) – bastard! (*He runs over to a bookshelf and throws loads of books off.*) Bastard! (*He starts to trash the place.*) What about me? . . . Fuck you, Brother Kiyi . . . What about me?

As he is throwing the books all over the place, a bare-chested **Kwesi** *comes running down the stairs. He sees* **Carl** *wrecking the joint.*

Kwesi Carl! What the fuck are you doing?

Carl *clocks his state of undress. Does the maths.*

Kwesi What you doing?

Beat. While **Carl** *confirms the maths.*

Carl Who is that?

Kwesi What?

Carl Who's upstairs with you?

Kwesi What you talking about?

Carl I said who's upstairs with you, Kwesi?

Kwesi No one.

Beat.

Carl Is Alice up there?

Kwesi I don't know what you're talking about, but I figure you're losing your mind.

Carl But you don't even like her, Kwesi?

Kwesi Don't worry about what I like, you need to be . . .

Carl *makes to go upstairs.* **Kwesi** *blocks him.*

Kwesi Where you going?

Carl Get out my way! I need to talk to her.

Kwesi You ain't got no business up there . . .

Carl Yes I have. This place still belongs to Kiyi, you know?

Kwesi Ah-hah! But right now that's my space.

Carl Then why couldn't you settle with that? Why you gotta have everything, Kwesi?

Kwesi Carl, I'm not going to tell you again.

Carl *makes to head upstairs again.*

Kwesi Carl, didn't you hear me?

Kwesi *pushes* **Carl** *back.*

Carl   I wanna see if she's alright. Alice would never willing go with man like you. Never!

Kwesi   Did you hear anyone screaming?

Carl   That's exactly what I heard! Alice . . . Alice, it's alright, I'm coming. I'm coming to save you . . . I'm coming.

He runs towards **Kwesi**. **Kwesi** *tries to grab him; they struggle.*

Kwesi   I . . . told . . . you . . . to . . . calm . . . the . . . fuck down.

Eventually they land on the floor.

Carl   Ahhhh, why you got to take everything? Ahhhh!

Kwesi   Calm down, Carl.

After a bit, **Carl** *escapes* **Kwesi***'s grip.*

Carl *(screams)*   Touch me again and I'll kill you. My mother always used to say a liar can be a thief and a thief can be a murderer and that's you. Think I don't know what you doing? I heard you and your boys last night.

Kwesi   What you talking about?

Carl   You, you stolen from me. You're stealing from Kiyi.

Kwesi   I didn't steal nothing from no one.

Carl   Yes, you did. It's not no Turkish boys taking over the store, it's you. You and your Somalian brothers.

Kwesi   That's rubbish!

Carl   I heard you, man. Don't tell me what I heard.

Kwesi   Who you gonna believe, me or your lying ears? You sure you weren't taking drugs when you heard that?

Carl   How could you do that to Kiyi? After all he's done for you!

Kwesi   After all he's done for me? Kiyi ain't done nothing for me. What Kiyi does he does for himself. Is it my fault he can't run his affairs? Did I make him default?

Carl   You bastard.

He runs at him again. They struggle.

Enter **Brother Kiyi** *and* **Norma***, unseen by the boys.*

Brother Kiyi   What the . . . My books, what's happening?

He runs over to the boys and tries to separate them.

Brother Kiyi   Boys . . . what the hell is going on? Boys, stop this!

Norma   What the arse!

Carl   It's him, Kiyi, him! You have to kill the enemy!

Brother Kiyi   What you talking about?

Carl   The traitor. Know who's gonna take over the shop on Monday? Him and his boys.

Brother Kiyi   Pardon?

Carl   That's right. That's the kind of man he is, Kiyi. A thieve!

Brother Kiyi   Carl, calm down. What kind of behaviour is this, boys?

Carl   Will somebody for once listen to me! I've seen the boxes of perm juice. Ask him, Kiyi, ask the ginal!

Brother Kiyi   Kwesi, what the hell is he talking ab −

Kiyi *looks at* **Kwesi***. He sees the truth in his eyes.*

Beat.

Kwesi   It ain't just like that, Kiyi, I was going to tell you . . .

Brother Kiyi   Tell me what?

Kwesi That, well, well yeah, we, what was we going to do, Kiyi, mek Dongol buy it?

Brother Kiyi When was you going to tell me – when I walked passed and saw the wigs in the shop window?

Makes the decision to go softly front foot.

Kwesi How many times have I talked to you about opening the place out, Kiyi? People don't – want – books. They wanna party, and look good, have the latest hairstyles, and nails and tattoos. That's where niggers be at, Kiyi. They ain't spending they money in here. Why should the other man take our money, Kiyi? That's why we powerless, 'cos we ain't where the money at.

Brother Kiyi It ain't about money!

Kwesi That's why you're on your knees picking up books people haven't bought, innit? Where's the respect in that?

Brother Kiyi Selling Afro Sheen gonna get you respect?

Kwesi It's gonna get me into the position that when you want to renew your lease you come to me! Five years from now Afro Sheen gonna buy us a next store and a next store and a next. Before you know it we got all of this place! And *that's* when the revolution really starts.

Alice *enters. She is still slightly dishevelled.*

Alice That's right. (*Public Enemy song.*) Fight the power!

Kiyi *looks at the topless* **Kwesi**.

Carl Alice, are you OK?

Alice I'm great!

Brother Kiyi *glances at* **Norma**. *She stares at him. He looks away, embarrassed. No one knows what to do or say. It all slowly dawns on* **Carl**.

Carl Nooooo! (*He runs out of the store.*)

Alice *stands by the desk.*

Brother Kiyi *slowly bends down and starts to pick up the books.* **Norma** *helps him. He suddenly see's that the photo-album box is empty. He looks around and spots that the album is on the desk. As he picks it up,* **Alice** *places her hand on it.*

Alice   Are these pictures . . .?

He doesn't let go.

Brother Kiyi   Private.

Alice   Is that so?

She pulls it from his hands. **Alice** *opens the album and points to the picture on the first page. It's of a six-month-old baby girl.*

Alice   What a cute baby! Who is this?

Brother Kiyi *doesn't answer.* **Alice** *turns a page.*

Alice (*a little more intense*)   Who is this, right here? The one with the ribbons and the silly dress?

He still doesn't answer.

Alice   Aren't you going to answer me?

Norma   Um, Kiyi, don't take this, don't let the young girl talk to you so!

Brother Kiyi   Norma, could you go and see to Carl, please?

Norma   I'm not leaving you!

Alice *runs and grabs a picture out of her bag, and shows the photo album.*

Alice   You see this? This is the only picture I have of me as a child. Cheeks are a bit bigger, but hey! They look a lot alike, don't they?

Brother Kiyi *remains quiet.*

Alice   So I ask again, I wanna know who this is in the album? (*Checking the reactions of* **Norma** *and* **Kwesi***, who has been silently watching.*)

Brother Kiyi (*stubborn*)   You already know, there's no need
for me to . . .

Alice (*explodes*)   Yes, there is a need! (*Calms.*) I need you
to say: Alice, this is you. This is the child I gave away, this
is the child I had and then couldn't be bothered or be arsed
to look after, so I dumped into some children's home to fend
for herself, away from anything or anybody that cared, away
from anyone that looked or sounded like her, away from all
that is kin and natural and safe and you're a fucking fraud,
Peter Allan, whatever you call yourself now, fucking Brother
Kiyi. You're a fraud, just like your fake fucking books.

Brother Kiyi   They're not fakes!

Norma   Who is this girl, Kiyi?

Brother Kiyi   Norma, let we talk later, na?

Norma   Who is this girl?

Brother Kiyi   I don't know, alright!

Alice (*screams*)   You don't know! You're more concerned
about your stupid friends than you are about me, standing
here before you begging to be named, recognised.

He stops in his tracks.

Brother Kiyi (*trying to be together*)   You're not begging to be
recognised. You know who you are!

Alice   I do, do I?

Brother Kiyi   Yes, otherwise you wouldn't have come here
to play with me. To test me.

Alice   I came to see why I look the way I do. Why I cross
my legs when I'm afraid. Why I talk and smell different
from all around me. I came to see why I was the one that
was battered and bruised and taken. And what did I find, a
sad, old, hateful man who pretends to unearth the truth, but
houses lies! Where's the sense in that?

Brother Kiyi   Oh, go on! Any more? What is this I hate?

Alice   You hate everything! Yourself, your life, your people!

Brother Kiyi   My people?

Alice   Yes, you hate your people more than anything else. *I* see you when you speak of them on the phone, you curl your lip.

Brother Kiyi   Everyone will tell you I'm the father of this area. Norma, tell her.

Norma   I can't tell her nothing, Kiyi, I don't know who she is.

Brother Kiyi   I have sacrificed my life to educate them of their history, their heritage . . . (*He stops himself.*)

Norma   Is that you daughter?

Alice   Well, you've failed, failed, failed, that's why you hate them.

Brother Kiyi   I do not hate. I'm disappointed, maybe. Hurt possibly, but I don't hate. I love my community. I built this for my community.

Alice   You're making me want to throw up! What do you know about love? You leave your child to rot, to be raised by the very people you are trying to educate your community against, and you talk about love? What did you build for me?

Brother Kiyi   I'm not educating my people against anybody. I was teaching them to love themselves.

Alice   (*new idea*) Was it these? (*Pointing to the books.*) Are these the reason? Was it too much to have a child like me and do all of that? Is that what it was?

Brother Kiyi *doesn't answer.*

Alice   'Cos if it was, you're wrong, see. You're wrong, 'cos we are the future. We are where it's at. You're borrowing from us and you don't even know it. (*She runs to the shelves and starts pulling down books.*) See, Bob Marley, mixed race.

Alexandre Dumas mixed, and she's mixed an' he's mixed.
Most of your so-called black heroes are mixed. All of us are
mixed!

Brother Kiyi There's a difference between being mixed
and mixed race.

Alice You fascist bastard. I AM YOUR CHILD, and
you're distancing yourself from me?

Brother Kiyi I'm not distancing. I'm . . . you know, that's
exactly what your mother would do to me. Twist me up.
Lose her temper and start to scream, and I wouldn't know
what to do. It's her spirit in you, innit, come to haunt me.
You come to haunt me, Chantella?

Alice My name is Alice!

Brother Kiyi Your mother named you Chantella.

Alice Chantella? Why would my mother give me one of
those made-up black names? Why would she succumb to
that? Why would she even lay with a beast like you? You
forced her, didn't you? You took her, right? That's what you
did, you forced yourself on my mother and she had no
choice but to marry you – she wouldn't have, I know it . . .

Brother Kiyi What the fuck are you talking about? What
do you know about your mother? You don't know nothin'!
You don't know what she took to be with me, what shit I
took just walking down the street, just fucking being with
her. What do you know? What do you know? What does
your blasted generation know? Do you have people spitting
at you in the street? Do you have shit smeared on your
windows because you're with someone that you love? No,
you don't have any of those things, so you just open your
mouth and let any old bullshit spurt out!

Alice (*matching rage*) I don't know anything because you
won't tell me!

Brother Kiyi (*screams from the heart*) What do you want me
to say? What do you want me to say?

Norma   (*does the math*) Alice, I would stop right now if
I were you?

Alice   (*shouts back*) I want to know why I don't have a
mother –

Brother Kiyi   Of course you have a mother.

Alice   – why I don't have a mother that's here, that wants
me?

Brother Kiyi   I don't know, isn't your mother down there
in Somerset or wherever you come from?

Alice   I want my mother back, I want my mother.

Brother Kiyi   Well, you can't have her because I killed
her, alright? Is that what you want me to say? Is that what
you want? I – killed – her! There! I've said it.

As if all the energy has been drained from her, **Alice** *stands and
simply stares at* **Brother Kiyi**. *All his energy has suddenly gone as
well.*

Brother Kiyi *looks between* **Alice** *and* **Norma**. *Although*
Norma *had just worked it out, she has never heard* **Brother Kiyi**
say that before.

Norma *steps towards* **Alice** *to embrace her.*

Norma   Oh child . . .

Alice *quickly steps back.*

Alice   No, don't . . . don't.

Beat.

I feared that. I want you to say something else. Something
other than . . . (*She exhales as if punched in the stomach. She begins
to retch.*) Oh Jesus, why did I do this?

Brother Kiyi *makes his way towards her.*

Alice   Don't you dare!

Alice *runs out of the shop.* **Norma** *looks at* **Brother Kiyi**, *and
then follows after her.*

Norma   Alice!

Silence.

Eventually **Brother Kiyi** *looks at* **Kwesi**, *who has been standing there taking this all in. They don't know what to say to each other. Eventually* **Kwesi** *attempts to speak.*

Kwesi   I . . .

But **Brother Kiyi** *jumps straight in.*

Brother Kiyi   Shhhhhhhh! Please! Just leave, Kwesi. Leave.

We get the sense of absolute danger as **Brother Kiyi** *looks to the door.* **Kwesi** *understands.*

Kwesi   I didn't know she was your daught . . .

Brother Kiyi *stares at him.* **Kwesi** *leaves.*

Brother Kiyi *picks up the photo album and places it neatly on the desk.*

Lights down.

Scene Six

Fix Up Bookstore. Saturday evening.

The shelves of the bookstore are half-empty. Boxes are neatly placed at the side. All of the sculptures are down, as are the paintings.

Brother Kiyi *is sitting in the middle of the store. He is both physically and mentally in a world of his own. He has a narrative book in his hand, not aware of the happenings around him.*

Carl *and* **Norma** *take the remaining books down off the shelves, the boxes off the floor, and either carry or wheel them out to the waiting van outside. In and out they go as fast as they can – almost at double speed if we could get it. As they work they speak narratives from the books.*

Norma   'Me modder name was Lucindy. Heard de odder negroes say she was a good woman but she died when I was a little boy. Not more than three or four. She left me likkle brodder 'bout eleven, twelve months old. I can remember a little her dying. She'd rock me in she arms and sing, "Lord all I have is deeeee"!'

Carl (*taking James Baldwin's* Notes on a Native Son) 'Neither white nor blacks for excellent reasons of their own have the faintest desire to look back. But I think that the past is all that makes the present coherent . . .'

Norma (*taking Maya Angelou*) 'I am phenomenal woman . . .' (*She takes one of the slave narratives.*) 'Slavery days, man dey was hell. Ain't nothin' you folk are gonna tell me to convince me odderwise . . .'

Carl 'And some Negro leaders further believe that by the amalgamation of black and white, a new type will spring up, and that type will become the American and West Indian of the future. This belief is preposterous . . . I believe that white men should be white, yellow men should be yellow, and black men should be black . . .'

The following audio cassette recordings gradually fade up.

Voice of Claude If we must die, let it not be like hogs hunted and penned in an inglorious spot, while round us bark the mad and hungry dogs . . .

Voice of Baldwin Now, we all knew. I know you knew, and I knew too, that a moment was coming when we couldn't guarantee, that no one can guarantee, that we won't reach the breaking point, you know?

Voice of Marcus Should I openly help improve and protect the integrity of the black millions or suffer? I decided to do the latter. There is no future for a people that deny their past!

We hear **Alice**'s *voice, even though she is not present. At the peak of the narratives we blend in an eclectic mix of Marcus Garvey, James Baldwin and Claude McKay.*

Alice Even with my good treatment, I spent most of my time planning and thinking of running away. I could have done it easy but but my old father used to say, 'No use running from bad to worse.'

By the end of this sequence the shop is nearly clear of all boxes except the two that **Brother Kiyi** *is sitting on.*

As the sequence has progressed, we have seen **Brother Kiyi** *stand on the box, place a tie around a beam and look through the loop, before sitting right back down again. Not able to do it.* **Brother Kiyi** *then goes to his desk, pulls out a knife. Almost a prayer.*

Brother Kiyi   Oh Marcus, why could I not be like you, why could I not have had the strength that you had? Why did your spirit not choose me?

He slowly starts to chop off his locks. When they have all gone, he runs his hands through what remains of his hair. His hands eventually fall on his face. He screams.

Brother Kiyi   Ahhhhhhhhh!

He pulls himself together.

Norma *re-enters the shop.*

Norma   Kiyi, you OK?

Brother Kiyi   Yes. Fine.

Norma   Well, everything done. Peter waiting to go. What we can't fit in yours we'll put in my garage. You coming?

Brother Kiyi   No, I'll walk home if that's alright.

Norma *stares at* **Brother Kiyi**.

Brother Kiyi   What?

Norma   What do I do with all that I have learnt from you, Kiyi? If even *you* peddle lies, who can I trust?

Brother Kiyi   I don't know, Sister Norma.

Norma   I go see you.

Brother Kiyi   Yes.

Norma *leaves.*

Brother Kiyi *returns to sitting on the boxes. He begins to sing the blues slave chant 'Adam' to himself. Very slowly, void of emotion.*

Brother Kiyi   Ohhhhhh Eve, where is Adam. Ohhhhhh Eve, Adam's in the garden picking up leaves.

Enter **Alice**.

Brother Kiyi *(without looking at her)*   An old slave chant from the Deep South.

Beat.

I would offer you a book to read but I don't expect you will be staying here that long?

Alice   No.

Brother Kiyi   I like that. No more questions. Statements are clean, you know where you stand with them, don't you?

Silence.

Brother Kiyi   It was an accident, you know . . . I didn't mean to . . .

Alice *puts her hand up to stop him.*

Alice   Please . . . I . . .

Brother Kiyi *retreats. After a few beats, he can't resist it.*

Brother Kiyi   There was so much pressure, Alice. So much hate, do you know what that does to your humanity? It shrinks it. It crushes it.

Alice *doesn't answer. After a few beats,* **Brother Kiyi** *realises that it is pointless trying to explain. He picks up the photo album and brings it to her.* **Alice** *opens it and looks at the picture of her mother.*

Alice   All of my life I have looked like no one. Until now.

Brother Kiyi *stares at her, confirming the truth that she does look like her mother.*

Alice *puts the photo album to her chest.*

Alice   I suppose I've got what I came for, right?

Brother Kiyi *nods.*

Alice   I really want to hate you, Kiyi. Part of me even wishes you weren't losing the store, but actually I think it's only fair, right, just that your castle tumbles and falls.

Silence.

Brother Kiyi   I built it to shut out the noise. Of you.

Alice *takes that in.* **Brother Kiyi** *stands up, looks deep into* **Alice**'s *eyes and walks out.*

Brother Kiyi   Thank you.

Alice *is left alone in the store, still clutching the photo album.*

The lights go down.